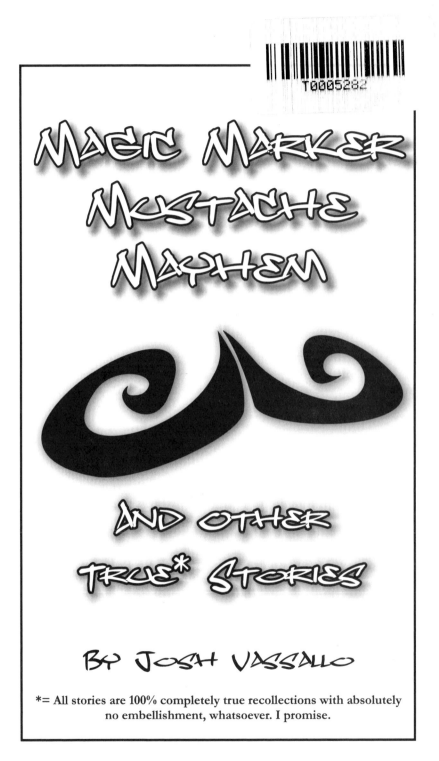

MAGIC MARKER MUSTACHE MAYHEM

AND OTHER TRUE* STORIES

BY JOSH VASSALLO

*= All stories are 100% completely true recollections with absolutely no embellishment, whatsoever. I promise.

THE SMALL PRINT BEGINS HERE . . .

THE DISCLAIMER . . .

All of the "true" stories in this book are nothing more than wild delusional fabrications of events that may or may not have ever happened. Anything in this book that remotely touches on anything that's even slightly true is more than likely an accident.

COPYRIGHT INFO . . .

First Edition, Second Printing

ISBN 097799260-8

PUBLISHED BY

MUSTACHE MAYHEM ENTERTAINMENT
COLUMBIA, SC

Visit us on the web at www.mustachemayhem.com

FOR MY MOM . . . YOU'LL SEE WHY.

SPECIAL THANKS . . .

I would like to thank everyone who helped make this book a reality. Most specifically, I would like to thank: my family, for their unconditional support in all of my endeavors, my lovely fiancée, Erin, for putting up with me while I was working on this book, and my friends, Damon Sipe, Troy Fields, Drew Brashier, Lee Nelson, and Jeff Lawson for providing the inspiration for many of the characters in these stories.

I would also like to thank Virginia Dumont-Poston, for pushing me to write in the first place, and Nicholas Meriwether, for sharing his invaluable expertise of self publishing. Last but not least, I would like to give a big thank you to Theresa O'Hagan for proof reading my comma splice ridden disaster of a manuscript.

True Stories

Magic Marker Mustache Mayhem

To put it kindly, D-Love was "unique." Out of all of my numerous roommates over the years he had to have been the most "unique." Everything was a mystery with him and he went to great lengths to keep every aspect of his life as private as humanly possible. He spent nearly every waking moment with his girlfriend and he made every effort to keep their relationship a secret. In our two years as roommates, he never talked about her. He never remotely hinted at the fact they were together. He never even so much as told me her name. And when they finally got married, he even purposefully omitted her name from their wedding program just to keep the mystery alive. Seriously, he's that mysterious.

I never understood the need for secrecy, especially when I saw his girlfriend on a daily basis. Of course, the most I would see of her was when she scurried through the front door and down the hallway to D-Love's room, where they locked themselves in all night and never came out. It seemed like the only time he would leave his cave to see the light of day was to go out and buy massive amounts of DVDs to add to his already enormous collection.

DVDs were perhaps the only thing D-Love coveted more than his girlfriend. Well, his DVDs and his computer, which I wasn't allowed to touch either. His DVD obsession wouldn't have been so strange had he actually watched them. But he didn't. Instead he just bought countless numbers of DVDs, bagged them in mylar as if they rare comic books and then stashed them away in a gun safe equipped with custom shelving that he affectionately referred to as "the vault."

On numerous occasions I tried to explain to D-Love that bagging DVDs in mylar was just plain nonsense. But trying to talk sense into him was a pointless gesture. He would hear none of it. "Never question a Korean Cowboy," he would always say. Then he'd give me the old evil eye and continue bagging away. And then once "the vault" was locked down he would proceed to give me his usual forty-eight minute lecture on why I'm not allowed to touch his stuff.

These lectures always ended in the same manner; with D-Love pulling a magic marker from his pocket, waving it in my face and threatening, "Don't give me a reason to use this, Mac! Because I will! You know how daddy rolls!" I never was entirely clear on why the threat of drawing on my face with a marker was supposed to be intimidating…but it was. That being said, I never once took it upon myself to touch his DVDs. I did however ask on occasion how his collection was coming along. I always hoped that a day would come when he would lighten up and say "Oh, you want to check out the collection? Go right ahead. Heck, watch any DVD you want. What's mine is yours, Mac." But that day never came.

Instead, D-Love did whatever he could to keep the contents of his collection under wraps. He rarely mentioned any of his purchases and he always bagged them and stashed them into the vault as soon as he could. But despite his penchant for secrecy he did slip up a few times and mention his affinity for the *Evil Dead* trilogy. Not to mention he received an *Army of Darkness* fan club newsletter in the mail every month.

Aside from his prized *Evil Dead* trilogy, I had very little idea what movie titles he even owned. That fact absolutely killed me. Not knowing what was in the vault ate away at me at times and I con-stantly wondered what all the fuss was about and whether or not the collection lived up to the hype. But ultimately I became comfortable with the fact that I'd never know… unless D-Love went out of town of course.

Then one day as fate would conveniently have it, D-Love took an impromptu overnight trip to Charleston with his girlfriend.

With his bags all packed, as he headed for the door, he offered up a heart felt farewell, wishing me the best of times while he was away. Well, actually his exact words were "Touch my DVDs and see what happens." Sure it wasn't exactly the most uplifting of goodbyes, but it still gave me a warm and fuzzy feeling of camaraderie nonetheless. After all, I knew in my heart that what he really meant to say was "Fair thee well, dear Mac. I'll miss you my friend." Not to mention, I was voted "most optimistic" back in high school so I felt obligated to live up to my peer-appointed title.

With a firm warning in place, D-Love hit the road with an air of confidence and a sense of certainty that his scare tactics would keep me far away from his precious DVD collection… his "babies," as he called them. Not to mention he'd locked the vault and swallowed the key earlier that morning, ensuring I'd have no possible way to mar any of his pristine condition DVDs with so much as a fingerprint. However, despite his anal retentive efforts to keep me out, D-Love grossly underestimated my lock picking abilities. Well, actually, no, he was pretty dead on in judging my skills. I couldn't pick the lock to save my life and the whole experience ended quite miserably with several inexplicable grease fires.

After extinguishing the last of the flames I finally realized I'd never break in to D-Love's seemingly impenetrable vault on my own. It was then that I decided to throw down my hammer as well my assortment of chisels and call a locksmith. Since I had never called a locksmith before, I wasn't entirely sure what to expect. I did however have the preconceived notion that a locksmith would be phenomenal at picking locks, hence their title. That being said, I was more than pleased when I found an advertisement in the phone book that read "*Phenomenal Locksmiths* . . . 'We're phenomenally phenomenal!'" And oh were they ever "phenomenal."

After three and a half hours of patiently waiting for the locksmith who'd "be there in five minutes," there came a rapping, gently tap tap tapping on my chamber door. At that moment I swore to myself I'd never reference Poe again, but that's neither here nor there. Rather what's important was that I answered the door to find a short, scummy looking guy in a dirty tank top and torn jeans standing on the other side.

"You call a locksmith?" he asked. I was staring at the stains on his shirt too intently to answer him in time, so he answered his own question. "Well, that's me. I'm the locksmith. Friends call me Squirrel," the scummy looking man said with a smile as he stuck out his hand.

As I shook his hand I had to ask, "So… you're phenomenal?"

"Yup. Phenomenal, bo," he replied before asking, "where's your crapper?"

Something to the tune of eight flushes later, Squirrel emerged from the bathroom and it was then that I learned he was quite "phenomenal" indeed. I also learned that "phenomenal" was another way of saying "undoubtedly high on methamphetamines." After spending a few minutes chasing his imaginary tail, Squirrel then explained how the government sells his hair on the internet to fund alien rescue missions.

Crazy as he was, Squirrel was still able to crack open the vault with nothing more than an ordinary table spoon in less than thirty seconds, proving he truly was a phenomenal locksmith just as promised in the phone book advertisement.

Once I paid Squirrel in cough medicine, which I was never completely comfortable with, he went on his merry way and I was finally granted the once in a lifetime opportunity to peruse the mother of all DVD collections at my own leisure. Since it was the first and last time I'd ever have access to the collection, I wanted to make it count. With that in mind, I went straight for D-Love's prized possession; his *Evil Dead* trilogy.

While D-Love was busy chauffeuring his little lady around Rainbow Row and likewise "exciting" tourist attractions I fell into a blissful haze as I watched the hero, Ash, slay Deadite after Deadite, spouting classic one-liners all the while. The hours flew by like minutes. The concept of "sleep" lost all meaning. For what must have been years, well, hours, I laid on the couch, ate pudding and watched the entire trilogy, twice. Once in English and once in Portuguese. Sure, I didn't speak Portuguese, but the option was there and I wanted to take full advantage of the situation. The entire time I fast forwarded, rewound, paused, stopped and played at my convenience without fear of repercussion for "wearing out" the remote. It was quite simply the greatest night of my entire life.

But the next morning, I paid for it with interest. At five after eight I woke up to the sound of my alarm, which had been buzzing that annoying alarm clock buzz since six thirty.

"Damn you, Boomstick." That's all I could think in my tired little mind. "Damn you to hell."

On a normal day, I would set my alarm for six thirty. I would hit the snooze every nine minutes until it got to be about seven thirty. I found that the nine minutes between snoozes were the absolute best nine minutes of sleep you could get. If I could I'd bottle it up and sell it. Also, if I could, I'd try to make that last sentence make some sense. Regardless, waking up at seven thirty still gave me ample time to get up, brush my teeth, take a shower, get dressed and get out the door by eight so that I could make it to work on time.

Since I worked in a library, it was extremely important that I be on time. If I were even a second late, God knows what could happen. With out my watchful eyes and skillful hands, a book could be improperly re-shelved, disrupting the entire Dewey Decimal System, causing a chain reaction that would unweave the very fabric of the space time continuum and spin reality itself into a vortex of unorganized chaos, ultimately destroying the universe as we know it. Not to mention, my boss got totally pissed when I was late. He didn't yell or anything, but he gave me this wicked mean look . . . it was quite unsettling.

I hopped out of bed and ran for the bathroom. Well, I didn't really "run" so much as I "quickly shuffled" and by "quickly" I mean "slowly" and by "shuffled," I mean "crawled." As I crawled to the bathroom, I had just enough time to go through my mental checklist of what could and could not be done that morning.

When the numbers were all crunched, by my calculations, I had just enough time to brush my teeth, which was important, because the night before I stayed up late eating what I could only imagine was dog crap from the taste in my mouth. However I just couldn't fit the time for a shower into the equation.

So rather than being that guy that doesn't shower, I plotted out a brilliant scheme to mask my musk. I had decided that I would just wet my hair to make it look like it was wet from taking a shower. Then to eliminate the pure funk that I swear I could see coming off of me in green wavy lines, I sprayed on some cologne. It was the perfect crime.

When I got to work, everything was like normal. I went to my desk and started pretending like I was working, just as I did everyday. After a few minutes, one of my obnoxious co-workers walked by my desk just to smell me, as she usually did in the morning. She was one of those obnoxious women that had to sniff everything and make an elaborate production about how great everything smelled. Normally in the morning she walked by me and would take a ridiculously big breath and then let out an equally large exhale, coupled with an idiotic "ahhhhhhhhhh" at the end just to let me know she enjoyed it. Then she would yammer on about how I smelled like her boyfriend. But not that day. Oh no, not that day.

As she skipped, since she was the type of person who enjoyed skipping, up to my desk, I knew the massive "sniff" was coming. I also knew that, just like a blood hound, she'd smell right through my cologne bath and then she would know my dark horrible secret which she would tell, because that's what women do-they tell everything. If she told, then I'd be ruined. Ruined, I say!

Just as I suspected she approached the desk, waiting to inhale. She stood in front of my desk, just hovering above me as I sat in fear of being caught. My heart pounded a mile a minute as she drew her head back in order to take her overly dramatic deep breath. As I watched her nostrils slowly flare, my mind became a frenzy of unpleasant thoughts.

In a fraction of second, thousands of images and scenarios flashed through my head. I could envision her wincing back in disgust as she dry heaved. I could envision coworkers laughing hysterically behind my back. I could see them in the corners, whispering while they told their jokes. I could hear the jokes. I could feel the humiliation.

The sound of her nose taking in air was like a finger nails on a chalk board. I just couldn't take it anymore. It had to stop. In a desperate panic, I reached for the closet thing to me and lashed out against her, hoping I could some how side step fate and prevent the inevitable chain of events I had imagined from happening. This of course meant that I cracked her in the face with my keyboard.

She was out cold for just a few moments but when she came to, luckily for me, she had no recollection of what just happened.

"What happened?" she asked in order to prove my claim that she had no recollection.

"You fell." I explained.

"I fell? How did I fall?" she asked.

She was asking too many questions and it was freaking me out. Once again panic hit me like a ton of bricks. Eliminating the rationality of my conscience, my Id took over and it was my Id that smacked her again in the face with the keyboard.

This time she was out just a little bit longer than before, so I poked her until she woke up.

"You ok?" I asked.

"Uh . . . wha? what? Yeah . . . I . . . I feel fine," she said as she began sniffing, then added "damn, boy, you stink." She said, to which I replied with yet another keyboard to the face. That time she deserved it.

Once again she woke up with out a clue. This time she gave a big stretch followed by a sigh. "Mmm, I feel so rested," she said, just before receiving another smack to the face...that time was just for fun.

Over the next hour, I knocked her out at least 17 more times before she finally woke up and said "wow, you smell like my boyfriend." At that point, I gave a big sigh of relief. My plan worked. No one at work ever suspected that I hadn't showered that day, so that was pretty sweet.

The only down fall to knocking her out more than twenty times was that it broke my keyboard. Well, then of course, she did acquire slight brain damage from the experience and by "slight brain damage," I mean that as a result of the massive head trauma, the only phrase she could remember to say was "Wow, you smell like my boyfriend."

But that's neither here nor there. The more important point was that my keyboard was rendered useless. Without a properly functioning keyboard there was really no point of sticking around the library that day, so I took the rest of the afternoon off work and it was then that I realized that it's impossible to side step fate twice in one day.

When I walked in to my apartment, all of the lights were turned off and it was completely dark inside, as the absence of light tends to cause darkness, or so I'd been told. As I fumbled around, searching for the light switch, I heard the click of a lamp switch turning, followed by a bright light shining forth from the living room. I glanced over in the direction of the light to find D-Love sitting in the recliner, holding a black magic marker in one hand and a receipt that read "Phenomenal Locksmiths. We're Phenomenally Phenomenal," in the other.

"Why, hello, Mac," he said in a voice that would make Hannibal Lector wet himself. He glanced over to the receipt in his right hand then looked up to ask "Pfft . . . did you really think I wouldn't know?"

Before I could even defend myself or offer a plea bargain, D-Love flipped off the lamp, leaving me blinded. Through the darkness I could faintly hear light swishing sounds, signifying movement, just like in the movies when ninjas do their thing. A moment later, the lights were turned back on to reveal D-Love standing before me, holding a mirror in front of my face. Upon looking in the mirror I could see that I had a black magic marker mustache drawn on my upper lip. Then without a word, he tossed me the mirror and walked away.

-True Story. ౿ა

I Got Banned From the Multiplex

One morning, just as the sun crested the nearby hillside, flickers of light reflected off the dew covered fall foliage sending a bright crimson hued wave of light through my bedroom window. As the sun warmed my face I got out of bed and said a prayer, thanking god for yet another glorious day. I then went about my normal morning routine.

I drew back the curtains and opened the window to hear the splendid sounds of birds chirping. I was touched nearly to the point of tears by the sight of children innocently playing in neighboring yards. The sound of their laughter brought back memories of a simpler time. A time when a sandbox, lemonade, and mom's hugs were all you needed to be happy in life.

At that moment, I wished I could go back to that time and live their forever. However, my fond reminiscences were brought to a screeching halt when I noticed a small sparrow helplessly hobbling on the ground with a broken wing. My heart sank and I became filled with grief as I watched the poor handicapped sparrow attempt to fly.

I had no other choice but to take the bird inside. Using the insanely awesome veterinarian skills I had picked up from volunteering every summer at the local animal shelter, I set the broken bone and released him back into the wild.

After sending the happy little sparrow on his merry way, I continued with business as usual for a typical Saturday. This of course meant tidying up my apartment and calling the church to look for better ways to serve HIM and spread the gospel.

"Father, is there anything else I can do to help spread the word of the lord, our god?" I asked as I polished my crucifix.

"No Mac. Der be nuttin' left for ya to be doin'. You've done it all laddie," Father O'Malley replied.

"Surely I can do more, Father," I insisted as I placed the crucifix back above my bed. "What about the lepers, Father? Surely I can help the lepers."

"No, laddie, you've cured them all," Father O'Malley reminded me.

"But the Lord's work is never done, Father. Surley there's something I can do," I insisted.

After taking a long, deep breath, as well as a short pause to let me know he was truly "pondering" rather than just merely "thinking," Father O'Malley finally offered his advice. "Well, perhaps der is one ting, laddie ..." He trailed off towards the end of the sentence just to heighten the suspense and build up the anticipation of the insightful wisdom he was about to bestow upon me.

And it was then that Father O'Malley did something truly magical. He managed to bring intrigue to a level I never thought was possible by softly repeated his words, saying, "yes ... perhaps ..."

"Yes, Father?" I asked in utter fascination of what was next to come.

"Well ..." he began slowly in order to bring the suspense to a boil. "Maybe, just maybe, you could find a way to properly convey a stereotypical Irish priest's accent through written text."

Though perplexed as to why Father O'Malley would make such a strange request, I kept in mind that the Lord works in mysterious ways and I gave him my word that I would honor his wishes. "I'll do my best, Father ... I'll do my best."

"I'm sure you will, laddie," he confirmed; then quickly added: "They're always after me lucky charms!"

"What?" I asked, confused as ever.

"Nuttin'. I'm just obligated to say that so you know I'm Irish.... God Bless," he said, then hung up the phone, leaving no doubt in my mind as to just how Irish he truly was.

Knowing there was nothing more I could do for the Lord, I decided to bake cookies for the local orphanage because I'm just that nice of a guy. And, since I just so happened to have recorded the previous night's episode of Martha Stewart Living, in which she made chocolate chip cookies from scratch, with all natural ingredients, including sugar from the sugar canes in her garden, I had the perfect recipe to ensure the perfect cookies for the perfect little orphans to enjoy. It was perfect.

Smelling the freshly baked chocolate chip cookies made me oh so tempted to try one but, according to the Word of God . . . Well, a pamphlet I read one time at a gas station, falling into the temptation of indulgence was just as sinful as drowning puppies. So, not wanting to burn in hell as punishment for engaging in sinful acts, I decided to have a half of a whole wheat bagel with light cream cheese instead. Even though it was the healthy choice, I still felt naughty because apparently I had become a fourteen year old girl that cared about her caloric intake. However, I managed to work it off since after stuffing my face I did pilates for an hour then began my four hour yoga work out.

As I was focusing my chakras, in the middle of downward facing dog, I was interrupted by Buttons, my roommate at the time, with his friendly greeting- which consisted of him punching me in the kidney as he yelled in a deep voice "What's up, fat ass?"

". . . oh . . . my chakras . . ." I squeaked as just the faintest bit of blood leaked into my trousers.

Buttons sat down on my bed and knocked the dirt from his boots onto my sheets as he munched on a cookie and got crumbs every where. "These cookies suck!" he yelled as he hurled a half eaten chocolate chip cookie at my temple. "It almost wasn't even worth it to eat every last one of them."

As I wiped crumbs off of the side of my face, Buttons bragged about his morning. "Oh dude, you should have seen this retarded bird that I totally killed. It was all retarded and stuff. So I totally killed it. It was awesome."

". . . you killed my spa . . ." I began, only to be interrupted by

Buttons demanding I go to the movies with him. "Ba-Har! Let's go the multiplex and see *"The Ladies Man!"* he yelled as he head butted me, nearly breaking my nose.

As I drifted in and out of consciousness all I can recall is Buttons saying over and over again, "I can't wait to see *The Ladies Man*. Oh holy crap, that Leon Phelps is awesome! I want to be him so bad! I even went and got some *Courvoisier* and everything. Yeah... basically it's my idea to see this movie."

After I regained total consciousness I explained to Buttons that I would rather not see *The Ladies Man*. "Buttons, my friend, I would prefer not to see *The Ladies Man*, as I am I sure it won't be a good movie. The five minute skits on Saturday Night Live were torture enough, so I can't imagine how painful it would be to sit through a feature length film based on the pimping skills of Leon Phelps."

Obviously he didn't see my side of it, so he hog tied me with duct tape and made me sit through *The Ladies Man*. I thought it was a bit strange that at no point did anyone in the theater ever inquire as to why I was hog tied with duct tape, but I suppose it happens so frequently that it wasn't completely out of the ordinary. But the displeasure of being hog tied was nothing compared to that of watching the movie.

The film was painstakingly awful. It was poorly acted, inadequately written, and clumsily directed. The premise was weak, the jokes were ill-conceived, the technical flaws were numerous, and the resolution was defectively crafted. It was by far, the worst mistake ever put on film. However, despite its abundant imperfections, something about the movie struck Button's fancy.

"That movie kicked more ass than an ass kickin' ass kicker!" Buttons yelled as the credits rolled. He then jumped up and stood on the top of his seat, where he ripped his shirt off and began beating his chest. As he howled with delight, an usher for the theater asked him to calm down. In turn, Buttons calmed down. And by "calmed down" I mean that he punched the usher in the kidney and continued howling.

"I have big muscles and a hairy chest! I'm the ladies man!"

Buttons shouted as he continued flexing his muscles and beating his chest.

Moments later an army of ushers swarmed the room and beat Buttons senseless with their flashlights. We were then escorted off the premises and banned from the multiplex for life. But as they drug Buttons away, battered and beaten, he still managed to affirm his manhood, murmuring "I'm the ladies man… I'm the ladies man."

-True Story. ∾

THE GREAT BOWLING ALLEY NACHO ONSLAUGHT

One time I was at the bowling alley with my cousin Leroy. Though we were mainly focused on bowling, we still managed to put together some semblance of a conversation between frames. I can't recall the exact subject matter of that conversation, though I do remember bits and pieces. From what I recall, it mostly consisted of Leroy blathering on to no end about what constitutes a good chilidog. I of course only chimed in with an occasional "uh huh" while I pompously adjusted my monocle and thumbed through the *Wall Street Review* to check for fluctuations in the pork belly market. From what I understood, most well-to-do aristocrats perused the stock pages while eating nachos at a bowling alley, and who was I to defy the status quo?

As Leroy droned on incessantly about the importance of relish, I polished off my large order of nachos without ever even considering the slight possibility that perhaps, just maybe, ingesting two pounds of pure fat may have a negative impact on my delicate digestive system. However, when the rumbling and gurgling began, it dawned on me that greasy beef and bean nachos with extra cheese and jalapenos may not have been the most sensible snack choice for someone with Irritable Bowel Syndrome. I really should have considered the possibility that they may have been a tad bit unsettling as they rampaged their way through my digestive system, but as they say, hindsight is twenty-twenty.

As the rumbling in my stomach began growing louder, I was forced to make a choice. I could either use the men's room in the bowling alley or I could take the fifteen minute drive back to my apartment. If I chose to use the restroom at my disposal, then I'd be forced to employ "the hover approach" as to avoid catching crabs, herpes, Japanese butt slugs or whatever other ungodly afflictions were floating around that communicable disease infested cesspool the good people at *Bowl-A-Rama* so casually referred to as their toilet seat. But I just wasn't a big fan of the hover approach, since hovering above the rim was just too risky. After all, it left open the possibility for the splatter effect and the thought of that was just too much to bear.

The fear of hover induced splattering led me to one conclusion: I would have to drive fifteen minutes back to my apartment, so that I could relieve myself comfortably. And just like that the choice was made. Without so much as a word, I waved goodbye to Leroy and I tossed my bowling shoes to the clerk as I rushed out the door.

As I raced home to get to the bathroom, my stomach was churning and bubbling. My hands were sweating like crazy, which made it impossible to wipe the sweat off my face. But, like an idiot, I kept hopelessly whipping my brow, each time getting more and more sweat into my eyes. It was a miracle that I could even see the cars in front of me, which by the way, were driving at least twenty miles per hour slower than the speed limit, because they all knew that I desperately needed to get to the bathroom, so they felt the need to torment me.

I became convinced that several cars ahead of me, a trucker was on his CB radio saying "yeah, this is Big Dog, we got a guy that's gotta take a slam back here, so let's make his life hell. Over." It seemed like every big rig in the world was in my way, making it impossible to pass anyone. It also made me clench my cheeks tighter and tighter, because I knew it would be just that much longer until I could sit on my throne.

By the time I got off the freeway, I was subjected to stoplight after stoplight, each eternal in length. A lot of people don't know this but traffic cops can actually sense when a powerful dump is brewing, so just to torture you, they stop traffic to allow a flock of ducks to cross. Nonetheless, I endured these minor setbacks, because after all, I was gripping the steering wheel as tightly as possible which for some reason or another was the magic cure-all. But when the comfort of the safety grip failed to bring a halt to the pain that was shooting through my colon, I began to curse the food that I ate, not for any particular reason, but I liked to believe that by shouting "damned bowling alley nachos!" it would somehow make up for the fact that I was a grown man that was about to soil himself.

Then I began to realize the hopelessness of the situation and I started to laugh, which only made it worse. Then when the laughter stopped, I had to grit my teeth and try not to cry. At that point I began to question why God felt the need to punish me. Then I made empty promises much like when someone's had too much to drink and they swear that they'll never drink again. I swore to God that I would never eat food from a bowling alley again or I would quit smoking or something to that effect. Then I realized he wasn't listening to me, because the rumbling sound that just echoed seemed to be a bit lower in tone, signifying that it was no longer in my stomach. It seemed that it had worked itself deep down into the colon and I was moments away from ruining my pants.

This happened just as I was pulling into the driveway. And for some reason, despite the pain and cold sweats, I felt comforted that I made it home. As I put the car in park and took the keys out of the ignition I did it slowly, because at this point I realized God was looking out for me and that my prayer worked. It felt so good that I was touched by God that I promised myself I'd go to church, bright and early on Sunday morning. And right then a sharp, stabbing pain shot through my colon, causing me to shout blasphemous obscenities.

I jumped out of the car and ran for the door. Of course I couldn't get my keys out fast enough, which induced the world famous "Final Stretch Heavy Breathing." I knew that I was almost there, but I couldn't get too excited, or else I knew I'd blow it. But I got excited anyway. My eyes began to tear up with joy as goose bumps covered my entire body. My heart rate increased and the hairs on my neck stood on end. It was an exhilaration that couldn't be matched. I was so giddy, but all of that ended when I walked in and my roommate, D-Love, was in the bathroom.

D-Love had a habit of always locking himself in the bathroom at the exact moment I needed it. During our tenure as roommates, it seemed like he would never have to go unless I did. I was pretty sure that his sixth sense was detecting whether or not I had to drop a bomb. After all, he always knew when I had to go and he would beat me to the punch, just to make me sweat. Or at least that was what I assumed. It could have been purely coincidental, but that's neither here nor there.

I stood outside the bathroom door, clinching my stomach and moaning in agony, for what had to have been an eternity. All the while I thought of every thing in my power to keep from exploding. I tried my best to think of something relaxing and calming, but all that echoed in my head was "Hurry up! Hurry up! Hurry up!" Like a broken record that skipped and played over and over again in my mind, until I questioned my own sanity, the words "hurry up!" repeated themselves. "Hurry up!" became my mantra as I tapped my feet and nervously bit my lip.

Then all of a sudden the loop broke and my mind became free to wander. I began fantasizing about what I was going to do to D-Love if he didn't hurry up. I imagined kicking in the door and throwing him out of the bathroom. I even imagined kicking him out of the apartment. I had visions of laughing my head off while I threw his clothes out the window and set fire to his precious DVD collection. As a distinct image of D-Love dressed as a homeless wino, holding a change cup, popped into my head the bathroom door opened.

"Oh what's up, Mac?" D-Love asked as he stood in the door way.

"Get the hell out of the way!" I shrieked, but only in my mind. In actuality I just said "nothin', nothin'" as I pushed him out of the way and entered the bathroom.

Finally my time had come, for I was only seconds away from dropping the most massive load in the history of mankind. In a furious blur, I somehow managed to unbuckle, unzip, turn, and sit in less than a second's time. However, my quick maneuver was all for nothing, as there was no explosion to follow. All that waiting and waiting and then nothing happened. I expected a triumphant climax to my struggle. However, a cathartic purging of all emotional energy that would some how improve my soul would not be the case, rather I just sat there in waiting.

"What's going on? How could this be? I've never had to . . ." my train of thought was disrupted by the cannon in my colon that just went off; blasting out a bomb so powerful it broke the sound barrier.

"Oh dear lord!" my mind screamed. I then glanced down to check the status of the porcelain, which I was sure the massive blast had shattered or at least cracked. To my surprise, it held strong. "It must have been manufactured with fine Italian craftsmanship," I thought to myself before another blast caught my attention.

I clinched my fist as if for some unknown reason that would make it better in any way. I gritted my teeth and a tear formed in my eye as my colon blasted out wave after wave of violent diarrhea, each burst more torturesome than the prior. My face became red and my eyes felt as if they were going to pop out of my head. And once again I went back to cursing the food. "Damned bowling alley nachos!"

At just the point when I realized that my colon had beaten me and I was, sadly enough, a victim to its wrath, I succumbed to the dark side and embraced the pain and agony and I excepted the fact that I was about to die on the toilet. Then it was over. Just like that, in the blink of an eye, it was over.

At that moment, there was a flash of white light and all of life's mysteries were revealed. For in that moment, I was beyond life or death; I was just a pure abstract of pleasure. Then all of that was once again brought to a halt, when one last nugget slipped out, causing cool toilet water to splash on my backside. As the last drop of water trickled down, I promised myself that I would never eat bowling alley nachos ever again, as long as I lived.

-True Story. ❧

PRINCESS PERFECTION'S ROYAL CELEBRATION

A hawk flew into my room one morning. Since hawks don't normally fly into my room, I can remember the occasion quite well. I awoke to the sound of glass shattering and wings fluttering as the gigantic bird came smashing through my window. I glanced over to see that my fiancée, Fee, who made me call her that because she thought it was a cute abbreviation for fiancée, was still sleeping soundly . I then recall gently waking her to alert her of the situation and then very calmly and collectively getting out of bed to shoo the hawk back out the window. However, Fee, who was obviously groggy from sleeping, somehow confused my delicate actions with those of shaking her awake, jumping up on the bed, and screaming like a frightened little girl until the hawk flew away. She must have been really tired.

After the hawk flew back outside, I noticed that it left a note behind. Apparently this was a trained hawk, sent to deliver me a message. I picked up the note and studied it closely. It was a golden engraved invitation to be a guest at the royal celebration of Princess Perfection's second birthday, hosted by King and Queen Perfect at their home, the Perfect Palace.

For most two year olds, who have no idea what's going on anyhow, a typical birthday party is nothing too extravagant. For the most part, they simply consist of family and friends getting together to say "oh isn't she cute… here's a toy." However, for my brother, Mr. Perfect, nothing less than grossly extravagant would be had.

That being said, in lieu of cake and ice cream in the back yard, my niece was to have a renaissance themed royal celebration complete with a marionette theatre, a jousting competition, a band of singing minstrels, and a juggling jester.

For a moment I was afraid that it would be a bit awkward introducing Fee to my family for the very first time at such an eccentric event. Then I continued reading the invitation and realized I was completely right to harbor such a fear. Apparently we were to dress up in medieval attire, just as all guests in attendance would be required to don appropriate costumes for their prospective roles. I may have been more optimistic about the whole thing had I been assigned a decent character, such as a knight or maybe even a squire. I would have even been happy with just about anything, but as it turned out, I was assigned the role of "diseased leper" and Fee was to be my wench.

Even though I was a bit apprehensive about the whole thing, Fee still wanted to meet the family. So on the day of the Royal Renaissance Ball, we put on our hot, itchy, ragged burlap costumes and got ready to drive over to my brother's house. As I was picking up my keys, Fee looked at me curiously and asked "what's the deal with your shoes?"

Confused as to what she was referring to, I asked, "What do you mean?"

"Pookie," she began, even though she knew I hated that nickname, "they're white. You can't wear white shoes after Labor Day. True or False?"

"Oh, please. Nobody in my family is going to care. Trust me." I said flippantly as we walked out the door.

The drive to my brother's house should have only taken an hour but due to Fee's tiny bladder, combined with her love of lemonade, we had to stop every ten minutes, prolonging the trip to three hours in length. So after our three hour trip, we finally arrived at the royal ball and we were both blown away by the sheer majesty of the event.

My brother had transformed his house into a golden palace surrounded by a moat filled with sparkling mineral water and rose petals. The drawbridge was a rainbow . . . Just for clarity, it wasn't a rainbow colored drawbridge. It was an actual, honest to god, rainbow. I didn't even think that would be physically possible but somehow, with my brother writing a big enough check, the engineering team from NASA made it happen.

Inside, the Perfect Palace was like something out of a fairy tale. The main hall was decorated with finely woven silk tapestries that stretched from ceiling to floor, complemented by gold framed portraits of the royal family that had been commissioned just for the occasion and were so life like Jan Van Eyck would scream with jealousy. In the center of the room was a grand buffet table trimmed with the finest of delicacies- rack of lamb, fillet mignon, Beluga caviar, lobster tails, and things I wasn't cultured enough to even know about. At the head of the table sat the royal family- my brother, his wife, and my niece- all of which were dressed to the nines in bejeweled silk garments and their heads were adorned with diamond encrusted crowns.

As a stark contrast to my brother's obscene display of excessive overspending, the rest of my family showed up in typical fashion. This of course meant that they all brought their own food. Seriously, why wouldn't they? It was a catered party, so the obvious choice would be to bring your own food, just in case. My cousin Leroy brought a bag of *Crunchy Chips*. My dad brought a corned beef sandwich and my mom brought a fifth of tequila.

As we mingled with the guests and hobnobbed with the high society socialites, who were dressed like idiots, I got the feeling that perhaps, just maybe, if we mingled long enough I could avoid my family and I could shelter Fee from meeting them. But it was when we wandered over to the buffet table that I bumped into Cousin Leroy and was forced to introduce him to Fee.

Because I didn't want to get trapped into listening to another one of his brilliant film critiques, I attempted to usher Fee away from Leroy, as I introduced them. "Fee, Leroy, Leroy, Fee. Alright, bud, talk to you later," I said as I pulled her in the opposite direction. Though I tried my best to shield her from Cousin Leroy, he managed to thwart my efforts by halting us with the attention grabbing phrase "Dude . . ." followed by a pause.

It was the pause that caught my interest. I wondered if he could have actually been thinking of something nice to say. I wondered if perhaps a comment such as "nice to meet you, Fee. Mac's told me so much about you," or maybe even "welcome to the family," was about to follow. But it didn't.

"Dude," he began as he sucked his teeth, "what's with the white shoes?"

"What?" I asked, shocked that Leroy would even notice.

"Dude, everyone's talking about them. I can't believe you wore white shoes after Labor Day," he said as he rolled his eyes. He then added "oh, dude, before I forget. . ." and paused once more. At this point, I had less faith that a pleasant comment was on its way and as usual I was right as he informed us, "I just got this new Chuck Norris DVD boxed set."

Cousin Leroy was perhaps the only person on earth whose DVD collection rivaled D-Love's. However, the subtle difference between their collections was that D-Love seemed to be selective in his purchases, where as Leroy collected any old crap he could pull out of the five dollar bin at *Big-Mart*. Needless to say, low budget, straight to DVD, B rate action movies were the staple of Leroy's collection.

As he stood before us, dressed in a full coat of black armor, he shoveled fist sized shrimp cocktails into his crust-ache trimmed mouth with one hand while holding a plate piled so high it was toppling over with fine cuts of meats and cheeses in the other, yet he still managed to sandwich the bag of *Crunchy Chips* between his elbow and hip for safe keeping. And why wouldn't he have wanted to keep them by his side? He was gobbling down a few hundred dollars worth of shrimp and steak paid for on my brother's dime, so why wouldn't he horde a three dollar bag of *Crunchy Chips* that he brought from home?

As he sucked his teeth and began reviewing his most recent acquisition I began tossing around the idea of "accidentally" jabbing a shrimp fork into my thigh just to be able to excuse myself. Then by the time he got around to claiming that *Missing in Action III* was the most underrated Chuck Norris film of all time, I went ahead and poked my leg a few times but never managed to actually puncture the skin. I then regretted having worn jeans on this occasion. As I began cursing myself for not wearing a lighter pair of khakis that would have been easier to tear through with a shrimp fork, my mom stumbled up to my rescue.

"Leroy! Good to see you," she said just before taking a swig of Tequila straight from the bottle, which afterward she added "now get the hell out of my face so I can talk to my no good son."

By the tone in her voice, I could tell it wasn't going to be one of my mom's typical drunken rants. I knew by her tone that I must have actually done something to upset her. Without wasting anytime, she let me know what I'd done wrong.

"What the hell is this? You're wearing white shoes after Labor Day? Everyone's talking about it. You've disgraced the family!" she shouted then turned to Fee and added "but you look lovely. It's so very nice to finally have a chance to meet you." They then exchanged pleasantries and my mom turned back at me, glanced at my shoes and then once again sneered at me in disgust.

"Sorry, ma, I didn't think that anyone would notice," I tried to explain, but she would hear none of it.

"You're dead to me, boy," she said just before guzzling down the remnants of her fifth of tequila. Then, without warning, she smashed the empty bottle over my head. I never thought that a liquor bottle would shatter so easily, or that it could hurt as bad as it did, but I was wrong.

I only wish I could describe the sheer pain and agony that I felt when jagged shards of broken glass ripped through the flesh on the top of my head and embedded themselves into my skull. I also wish I knew what happened after that at the birthday party, but the concussion I received from the massive blow to the head made it difficult to remember my name at the time, let alone what was going on around me. However, from what Fee tells me, the rest of the evening was really quite lovely.

-True Story.

Turbo Wings and Shenanigans

When I was a poor foolish college freshman, my old roommate, Buttons, decided to show me the ropes by taking me to a little piece of heaven on earth called *Frank's Bar and Grille and Check Cashing Oasis. Frank's*, as it was abbreviated, was just one of those places. One of those places that were best described with the precursor, "one of those places." It was one of those no nonsense places that went along just fine without the frilly things that fancy schmancy restaurants boasted about. Things like "customer service" and "sanitary cooking conditions." It was one of those laid back places that didn't require the wait staff to sing cheesy songs, wear hokey uniforms, remain "legally sober," or wear shoes. Yeah, it was one of those places.

Frank's claim to fame, oddly enough, wasn't the stale aroma of cigarette butts and cheap house brand liquor. Though hard to imagine, it wasn't even the old world charm of the sticky, urine covered floor of the men's room that kept people coming back. No, it was the "World Famous Turbo Wing" that put *Frank's* on the map.

The Turbo Wing was truly a thing of beauty. It was, hands down, the hottest thing ever created . . . Or the hottest thing that ever evolved, depending on one's outlook. Since the recipe was a Frank's secret, I could only image that the turbo wing sauce was comprised of two parts nuclear hell fire mixed with one part gasoline for that extra burning sensation.

Basically, the sensation of eating a Turbo Wing would equate to eating a handful of habanero peppers while being sprayed in the eyes with police issue mace. From what I'd been told, for a while, Frank's provided the habanero and mace combo with fries and a drink for a pretty fair price, but they had to stop, what with the law suits and all.

On my first visit to *Frank's*, Buttons duped me into trying one of the Turbo Wings I'd heard so much about. Since it was my first time there, and I didn't know any better, I quickly chalked up the talk of the dreaded "killer" hot wings as rumor, folklore and urban legend. Not to mention, all I had to go by until then were the stories I'd heard from Buttons and he didn't exactly come across as the most trustworthy source of information in the world.

"Are these things as hot as they say?" I asked, pointing to the flaming skull that listed the Turbo Wings on the menu.

"Let me put it this way," Buttons began, "I'm the only man who's manly enough to man handle a turbo wing. Everyone else just cries like little pansies because they're just little pansies that can't handle it," he said before taking a huge gulp of beer and then adding "God, I'm so manly! Look at my manly muscles! Look at 'em! Yeah!"

As Buttons stood on top of the table flexing his muscles and growling like a dog, I got the feeling he was exaggerating, so I decided to sign the liability waver and order a Turbo Wing just to see, first hand, if they lived up to the hype.

I was feeling fairly optimistic until a man in an iron mask, wearing protective gloves, used an apparatus, which looked much like a broom stick with a plate bolted to the end, to deliver the wings to the table.

"May God have mercy on your soul, boy," the man in the iron mask said as he walked back into the kitchen. At that point I was, to say the least, a tad bit intimidated. Sitting in front of me, on the plate, was one single turbo wing. It was sizzling and popping as steam and heat rose from it. The smell alone caused me to sweat more than usual, which anyone could attest to being an unreasonable amount.

Upon my fingers making contact with the wing, just to pick it up, the nerves in the tips of my fingers were destroyed. My dreams of someday learning to read brail were also destroyed, but that's neither here nor there. With my finger tips burning, I fought through the pain and managed to pick up the wing long enough to bring it towards my mouth. When I got the wing close to my mouth, in anticipation of the first bite, my beard hairs were singed off. I stuck out my tongue to taste the slightest drop of sauce and I immediately began to cry like a baby.

As the horrific burning sensation in my mouth began to spread to my sinuses, my nose began to run and my eyes watered. My eyes began watering so badly that I had no other choice but to wipe them. This proved to be huge mistake. As I wiped my eyes, a bit of Turbo Wing sauce that was on my finger got into my eye. My eye swelled shut as I fell to the floor moaning and weeping uncontrollably. And as I lay on the floor in agony, with snot all over my face and my eyes swollen shut, Buttons, of all people, came to my aid. He offered some comforting words that helped me through that dark time in my life.

"Bahar! Quit being a pansy!" he barked as he punched me in the kidneys. Surprisingly, a stern shot to the kidneys didn't do a whole lot to numb the excruciatingly painful burning in my eyes and mouth.

After a few minutes of wallowing in agony, praying for death, the man in the iron mask came back out from the kitchen and into the dinning room, where he used his broomstick spatula to scoop me up off of the floor and toss me outside. While I lay in the gutter, sweating, shivering, and shaking like a crack head, I came to two realizations. The first being that the Turbo Wing did, in fact, live up to the hype and the second realization being that I owed it to myself to dupe some poor fool into suffering the same fate.

Lo and behold, a year later, it was my turn to dupe some unsuspecting freshmen into falling for this little culinary torture treatment. Finally, I would be afforded the opportunity to laugh at someone else's expense, which I'd heard was quite fun. I decided to take this kid named Bull, who was a short little guy that seemed to be excessively weak, giving me the impression that he would actually burst into flames upon tasting the turbo wing, so that we could all have a good laugh at him. But as fate would have it, no one laughed.

After all, no one could have possibly been prepared for what they were about to see.

Buttons and I sat there giggling like school girls as the plate of Turbo Wings arrived at the table.

'So these are supposed to be hot?" Bull asked, nonchalantly.

"Why don't you take a bite and we'll tell ya," I giggled.

Bull picked up a Turbo Wing and studied it closely. He stuck out his tongue in order to get a slight taste of what he was up against. Unimpressed by the heat of the Turbo Wing, Bull gave a cocky smile. The crowd, which all of a sudden appeared, was rendered silent as they watched in awe while Bull licked every last drop of the nuclear-hell- fire-gasoline-blend of turbo sauce from the wing. The crowd nervously waited for Bull to make a comment, granted the hot sauce hadn't rendered him speechless by burning a hole in his throat.

"Meh, not bad," he said.

The crowd gasped as he dared make light of the awesome power of the Turbo Wing. Women fainted, babies cried, and men shouted in outrage.

"I say, I say that boy is the devil!" shouted someone in the back who happened to have an appreciation for Foghorn Leghorn. The crowd then began to panic and a feeling began to sink into my stomach, signifying that total chaos was just moments away. But just then, moments before the storm, a voice of reason rang out, calming the crowd.

"Shenanigans!" a red headed stranger shouted, "I call shenanigans! Those aren't real Turbo Wings! They can't be!"

"Yeah, shenanigans!" another man shouted. Then the crowd began to turn on Bull, chanting "shen-an-igans, shen-an-igans, shen-an-igans."

"Shenagninans!" one girl yelled, causing a record, which happened to be playing in the background, to come to a screeching halt. Everyone stopped and stared at the girl, who blushed and attempted to say the word once more, this time sounding it out "shen-ag-inons? Shen-ag-ninons?" She then hung her head in shame, whispering "damn you, hooked on phonics."

33

"Shenanigans!" the red headed stranger yelled once more, drawing focus away from the blushing girl and back to the matter at hand. The crowd then began chanting again whilst waving their pitch forks.

Out of curiosity, I dabbed my finger into a small spot of sauce that sat on the edge of the plate. There was no painful searing of flesh, as there had been the previous year, giving me the impression that something was amiss. Since my finger tip hadn't burst into flames, I was nearly convinced the crowd was right. It had to be shenanigans. However, my inquisitive nature wouldn't let well enough alone, because at that point, I tasted the hot sauce. At first it was a bit sweet, peppery, but sweet. It was along the lines of a watered down Tabasco sauce. It could barely even be described as spicy. One thing was for sure, it was definitely not the same sauce that had tortured me the previous year.

"This isn't it. I'm calling shenani…" I began only to be cut off by the wave of remarkable pain that quickly made its way from my tongue to my brain. My eyes watered and snot ran from my nose. Once again I fell to the floor in agony, crying for mercy. "Oh dear lord, it's even worse than last year!" I cried, as the man in the iron mask scooped me up and threw me outside, where I once again passed out in the gutter.

Though I was unconscious and didn't actually witness it, from what I was told, after I was thrown out, Bull dipped the wing back into the extra sauce that was on the plate, licked it clean again, ate the chicken wing, took a shot of moonshine and then blew a fire ball!

The crowd was awestruck by what they had seen. Rather than laughing at some poor fool's agonizing defeat at the hands of a hot wing, they had witnessed a miracle. For the first time ever, a mere mortal had bested the hot sauce gods. An everyday average Joe had laughed in the face of death. From that moment onward, the legend of Bull "the fire eater" grew. He was immortalized with a plaque that hung on the wall at *Frank's* . . . until it was stolen a week later by a bitter, rival hot wing enthusiast.

-True Story. ❧

COUSIN LEROY
THE GRILL MASTER

A long time ago, I made of list of all the things I'd like to do before I die. Due to lack of creativity, the list was pretty standard. It had the good old standby's that everyone would want to do before they die, like actually being able to take a dump in peace without someone knocking on the door to ask if everything is ok and such other popular dreams come true. But since I knew that would never happen I also included some more probable activities on my list of hopes and dreams. Among these, were such magical experiences as having the privilege of standing around outside in the blistering, sweat puddle inducing heat of South Carolina in mid-July, while getting attacked by mosquitoes for hours on end while watching some moron feebly attempt to barbecue. And sure enough, thanks to my cousin Leroy, that fantasy became a reality.

On one particularly hot summer day, my cousin Leroy invited me over to grill out. This of course was Leroy's excuse for being able to show off his new grill, as Leroy loved to show things off. Every time he opened his wallet to purchase even the most trivial of gadgets or trinkets I just had to come over and see it. He would get so excited over even the smallest things. I recall once getting an urgent phone call at two thirty in the morning and having to rush over to Leroy's to see what all the fuss was about.

When I showed up, Leroy came to the door in his boxer shorts, just as calm and collected as ever.

"Leroy, you ok? Every thing ok?" I asked in a huff.

"Dude, check it," he instructed as he ever so proudly waved a candy bar in front of me. Not knowing what I was supposed to be impressed with, I inquired "That's what I came over here for? It's a candy bar, Leroy. What's so special about it?"

He sucked his front teeth then shoved the majority of his plump, meat hook hand into his mouth to fish out a small bit of nougat from his back teeth. Then after licking the nougat from his finger tip, he sucked his teeth again, and smacked his lips loudly as he answered, "Dude," he began, still smacking his lips, "it's the good kind." He sucked his teeth once more, "It's the one with more nuts in it."

It was at pivotal moments like that when I seriously questioned whether or not I was adopted. I never could understand how Leroy was my own flesh and blood, but that was what I'd always been told, so I had to believe it.

Though I only ever received the one late night phone call, typically I would get three or four calls per week from my cousin, as I would be subjected to endless updates to the status of his extensive DVD collection. Whenever Leroy purchased a new movie from the five dollar bin at *Big-Mart*, I was the first to know. He would spare no detail as he described, in depth, the contents of each DVD, including the full motion chapter menus, the various available sub titles, the director and actor audio commentary, and, of course, the deleted and alternate scenes.

Because his DVDs were his greatest source of pride, I felt obligated to humor him and allow him to show off his most invaluable titles, such as his ever-so-rare director's cut of the straight to video action film, *RoboNinja*.

Among all of the things my cousin has shown off over the years, the only possession of his I have yet to see is his magical bathroom scale which weighs him in at just under two hundred pounds. But that's neither here nor there. The important thing was that Leroy thought small. Something worth mentioning was the time he invited me over to see his new television set. When I walked in the door, he had a huge ear to ear grin on his face and I knew he was about to explode from having to wait to show it off. From the excited look on his face I was expecting a sixty inch big screen, so imagine my surprise when he pulled a TV out of his front pocket. It was a handheld watchman with a two and a half inch LCD screen. Sure it may have been the size of a cell phone, but it had a "flat screen" and that made it better than my normal, stupid, bulky twenty five inch television, obviously.

With that in mind, I have no idea why I was shocked to see Leroy's choice in grills. Rather than taking my advice and getting an outdoor propane grill that could have possibly been useful, he opted to go with a new, state of the art, top of the line, mini hibachi grill. The cooking surface on that bad boy was all of about three square inches. That, I'm sure, would allow plenty of room for cooking upwards of two thirds of a hotdog at any given time. Not to mention, the hibachi had a maximum capacity of nearly four bricks of charcoal, which would put out enough heat to cook those hotdogs at just a little above room temperature, for an approximate cooking time of about four hours per pound.

Words can barely describe the shear joyful emotion I felt when he unveiled his new grill. I was under the foolish impression that a hotdog could be microwaved in less than thirty seconds, leaving no need to stand outside under the scorching hot sun while mosquitoes sucked several pints of blood from my forehead. But thanks to Leroy's purchase of that handy little hibachi, there would finally be a way to prolong the process of cooking hotdogs, which meant my life long dream of sweating to death while grilling outside would at long last become a reality.

Since it would take several hours to cook the pack of hotdogs, we decided to pass the time with an engaging, deep and meaningful adult conversation. Well, basically it was me listening to Leroy explain, in great detail, his techniques for organizing his DVD collection. Long story short, he organized them alphabetically by genre. Not the most riveting conversation in the world, but it was a conversation, nonetheless.

As Leroy described the pros and cons of organizing alphabetically by genre versus limiting himself to organizing solely by title, I checked the hot dogs. They weren't even close to being done. I was almost certain that I could have held the pack of hotdogs in my hand and shear body heat would have acted as a more efficient cooking tool than the hibachi could have ever been.

As the hours began to blend together and time itself seemed to be non-existent, I began to grow weary from heat exhaustion and starvation. As I baked in the sun, the continual flipping of hotdogs became a necessity. Much like a hobo that stands on the corner and shuffles his feet to keep warm in the winter, I had to flip hotdogs to stay sane in the heat. I had a rhythm going, actually. I would flip the hotdogs, swat the mosquitoes, and then wipe the sweat from my forehead. Flip, swat, wipe, flip, swat, wipe, and flip. But no matter how many times I flipped, the hotdogs just wouldn't get done.

As I flipped, swatted, and wiped, my mind began to play tricks on me. While Leroy listed his DVD titles alphabetically, then again in reverse alphabetical order, I was sure I was losing it. Right in the middle of the list I faintly recall hearing him say something to the effect of "dude, I got a great price on ham salad at the grocery store." But the next thing I knew he was back to telling me all about his new special edition *RoboNinja* DVD. Just as he began listing the special features, I checked the progress of the hotdogs. Though the sweat was pouring so heavily into my eyes that I could barely see, I was almost certain they were done.

Just to make sure my mind wasn't playing another trick, I poked one of the hotdogs with a fork. It was done! It was actually done. Finally! It was beautiful. I felt like I had just given birth in the sense that I was physically exhausted but I was relieved and over-joyed to look down at the wonderful thing I'd helped to create, knowing it was worth the pain and sacrifice. At that point, I had honestly never wanted a hotdog so badly in my entire life.

I picked up one of the dogs and wafted the wonderful scent of charbroiled processed pig parts towards my nostrils to take in the glorious aroma. Just as I began to salivate uncontrollably and my body started tingling in anticipation of the first heavenly bite, Leroy snatched the hotdog from my hand.

"Dude, these are for Oakley. We're eatin' sandwiches," he said using a tone that would suggest he was reminding me of past information rather than dumping new information on me for the first time. Trying to process this new piece of information, I could feel my brain fizzing like a freshly poured soft drink. My left eye began spastically twitching and my neck convulsed causing my head to uncontrollably tilt to the side. The proverbial cork was about to pop. I was losing it and I needed to hear something rational to help keep it bottled in.

"Oak . . . Oak . . . Oakley?" I managed to ask

"Dude, yeah, Oakley. My girlfriend's dog?" Leroy answered, using an inquisitive tone in an attempt to jog my memory. I kept twitching as Leroy began piling the hotdogs into Oakley's dish. He then further explained, "Oakley's a picky eater. Yeah, he won't eat hot dogs that have been in the microwave. He only eats 'em if they're charbroiled."

Finding Leroy's explanation just a bit less than rational, I felt a slight sting in the back of my head. I distinctly remember hearing a flicking sound, as if a light switch had been turned off, when the entire left side of my body went numb. Though I was almost sure I was having a mild heart attack, I felt oddly at peace. Everything went into slow motion and in a nearly psychedelic daze, I mustered the strength to as ask "so what are we eating?" To which he aptly replied, "Dude, I told you that I got an awesome deal on ham salad, so we're having sandwiches." And just then, Leroy snapped his fingers "oh, I forgot," he said as he dug in to his pocket. After a few seconds of fishing around, he pulled a can of ham salad from his trousers and waved it in front of me. "Dude, check it. It's the good kind."

-True Story. ∾

Just Trying to Find Some Pants

Not too long ago, I went to the mall in search of a new pair of pants to wear to an engagement party being thrown for us by some of Fee's friends. The invitation said to dress "snappy casual," so Fee suggested that I wear a pair of khaki cargo pants to go with the pink shirt she had picked out for me. It seemed that was the only way I could achieve the lofty status of being both snappy and casual at the same time. Since all I owned were men's comfort fit pleated slacks, I had to venture out to the mall in search of cargo pants.

As I stepped into *The Trend*, I couldn't help but recall the time when, just before entering third grade, my mom took me out to *Wholesale Plus* for a little back to school shopping. I was hoping to get my hands on a brand new pair of parachute pants, so that I could be every bit as awesome as my brother, Mr. Perfect, who had a massive collection of parachute pants in a wide variety of colors, making him the envy of every kid in school, including myself. I thought that maybe, just maybe, if I could get the green and black parachute pants with orange zippers, then perhaps he would envy me for a change. I also used to think that when I was old enough, I'd own a machine gun, just like Rambo. I harbored these ludicrous notions because I was eight years old and I lived in a fantasy world.

In my little eight year old mind I imagined I could just get my mom to drive me to the mall, where she would buy me a pair of pants. However, in reality, I was a "husky" built kid and that complicated things. Being husky meant I was too fat for normal kid sizes, but not quite fat enough for adult sizes. Teetering on the line between kid and adult meant that I usually only had one choice in pants: men's comfort fit pleated *Slacks,* just a little big in the waist and mile too long.

I hated *Slacks.* My mom would always alter them herself, tucking the waist and cutting the extra material off the legs. Hemming them enough to accommodate my stubby little legs meant chopping them off just below the knee to create some sort of mutated capri pant/shorts combination. Essentially they looked like clown pants when I wore them and I hated them. I hated looking like a clown and I wanted desperately to look cool. As far as I could figure I would need parachute pants to make that dream a reality.

As we entered the junior department, I ran over to the display of parachute pants and started sifting through the pile until I found the exact pair I wanted; green and black with orange zippers; the epitome of awesome. I eagerly snatched them up and presented them to my mom. "These are the ones I want, Ma. Please, please, please, please, can I have 'em?"

My mom of course knew that my "husky" status would eliminate any possibility of actually being able to squeeze into the pants I so adored. So, in an effort to spare my fragile young ego the devastating blow of harsh reality, she tried her best to deter my interest.

"You'll shoot your eye out," she warned.

"But Ma, they're just pants," I explained.

"Oh, right . . . well, parachute pants are for fags," my mom retorted.

Without heeding her warning on whether or not a pair of pants could determine sexuality, I grabbed the parachute pants and ran for the dressing room. I threw off my lame slacks and began to slip on the absolute sweetest pair of pants in the world. I kept thinking how awesome I was going to be at school the next day and how all the other kids would envy me. In my little fantasy world, all I needed next was a tattoo, a machine gun, and a snake and then I'd be better than Rambo. As I pulled the pants up, they became just a tad bit snugger with each inch they moved up. Soon, my circulation was getting cut off, but it didn't matter because they were cool, so I figured cool clothes were supposed to do that.

I tried my damnedest to button them, but for some odd reason the button was a good two or three inches out of reach from the loop. "Hmm… Something's got to be wrong," I thought. At that point my mom knocked on the dressing room door.

"You doin' ok in there, sweetie?" my mom asked.

"I'm fine," I explained, as I strained to pull the fabric closer together in the foolish hope that I could button the pants.

"I'm coming in," my mom announced as she burst through the door. It was at that moment that the waist in the pants gave in to all of my pulling and stretching and ripped apart.

So there I was with in my tightey whiteys with a ripped pair of parachute pants and the entire store could see me. It was a memorable experience to say the least. My mom came in and shut the door behind her. She then calmly explained as gently as she could without hurting my feelings that I was different than other kids and because of that I wouldn't be able to dress like the other kids.

"Now look what you did fat ass! You tore them . . . great . . . now I'm gonna have to pay for these!" she said as she surveyed the tear. "Just sit still while I'll get you some pants," she said as she exited the dressing room. I felt touched by my mom's tenderness.

A few minutes later my mom returned with my usual pair of men's comfort fit pleated *Slacks*. They were lame but, since I was "husky", I was stuck with them. On the first day of school, I wasn't the coolest kid in the world. I wasn't the envy of my friends. I wasn't tougher than Rambo. I was just a "husky" kid in *Slacks*.

Sixteen years later, standing in the middle of *The Trend*, leafing through countless pairs of size twenty eight pants, I realized history was repeating itself, except this time cargo pants were the unattainable object of my desire. I began to think I was destined to an eternity of forced brand name loyalty to *Slacks*, who it seemed was the only company on earth to manufacture pants large enough to accommodate my "husky" physique. However, my deep rooted hatred for *Slacks* combined with my desire to wear "snappy casual" pants wouldn't allow me to halt my search so easily.

I looked around for a sales associate, but as per usual, none were to be found. I finally spotted an anorexic looking metrosexual, with spiky bleached blonde hair and a highly manicured, pencil thin goatee, sipping on a café latte and standing near the counter. As I've grown accustomed to poor service, I was sure that this apathetic looking young man had to be an employee. Everything about him exuded that bitter hatred that comes from working as a second key shift leader at *The Trend* after five years of college. Not to mention he was donning an employee name tag that read "Chauncey."

As I approached the counter, Chauncey looked at me with disgust and aptly stated "Ok, chu-dunk-a-dunk, *Wholesale Plus* is on the other end of the mall, just past the food court." He then pompously stirred his coffee and added, "good luck at *The Steak and Fry Shop*," before taking a sip.

"Chu-dunk-a-dunk-dunk!" his coworker, Isaac chimed in. Then the pair exchanged high-fives as Chauncey exclaimed "Oh, snap! Best burn ever!" and then settled down to take another sip of his café latte. I wasn't exactly sure what any of that meant, but I was pretty sure they were insulting me, so I snatched the coffee from Chauncey and threw it in his face after kicking Isaac in the shin…in my mind. In reality, I defiantly took my business elsewhere. I never said revenge was my specialty.

After leaving *The Trend,* I ventured across the way to *Holster Co.,* which I'd heard was quite hip with the kids. Since I'm "down," I figured it was the best bet for finding something "wicked," "funky fresh," "dope," or "sick to death." However, walking into *Holster Co.* was like stepping into a scene from *Lord of the Flies.*

There were teenagers everywhere and without a doubt, they ruled the store. The only adult within eyesight was sitting at a desk, milling over paper work with an accountant as she prepared to take out a second mortgage on her home to pay for the obscenely overpriced, torn up, faded and shredded cargo pants her daughter just had to have.

I was clearly out of my element, but I was so enthralled with the hype that I decided to look into getting some of these faded, torn up, crappy looking cargos everyone was raving about. I walked over to the display and began searching for something in my size. Oddly enough, not one single pair of pants had a size indicated on the tag. I asked one of the sales associates if they could help me find a pair of pants in my size.

"Excuse me, Miss. Do you have these in a size 42?" I asked, pointing to the display. She paused from her cell phone conversation to give me a puzzled look.

"Uh, listen, I have to help some clueless old fat dude, so let me…" she told the person on the other line, right in front of me, with out even attempting to whisper. She then yelled in to the phone "I said he's totally old and fat!" She then looked at me and covered her phone to explain "oh, my bad, but her dad's like totally poor and can't afford a good cell phone, so you have to like yell at her so she can hear you." Then without missing a beat, she uncovered the phone and went back to her conversation " No! No, he's not like circus fat, he's just well, you know, he's like really fat! Anyhow, I gotta go! Call me every five minutes!" She then exclaimed "Holla!" and turned off her phone. She was then more than happy to explain the store's sizing policy.

"Like, we don't have those sizes" she said, emphasizing the word "those." She then flipped her hair and began a ninety mile an hour explanation of what sizes they actually did carry. "Like the only thing we have is the metro zero and that's like a women's zero but all the guys who shop here have to be able to wear that size too because that's all we have and that's why it's the metro zero because it's for guys and girls so that's all we have because like it's the metro zero and I don't think you'd fit in it but if you know someone who isn't fat then maybe you could buy them some of our shredded cargos cuz if they're not fat then they'll be able to wear 'em … " she then took her very first breath since she began chirping away and added "so anyhow, like *Wholesale Plus* is on the other side of the food court, just past *The Steak and Fry Shop*." She then waved goodbye and added "holla!" as she walked away, dialing another number on her cell phone.

So far for the day I was zero for two, but I still wasn't completely discouraged. I still held on to the belief that somewhere in the mall I would have to be able to find a pair of cargo pants that actually fit. However, after being turned away from *Banana Commonwealth, Canadian Eagle, Ambercrombie,* and several other stores with non-copyrighted names, I began to lose hope and began aimlessly meandering through the mall with no real sense of direction or purpose.

While wandering around I just so happened to pass an *Old Army* and like a lightening bolt it hit me: Cousin Leroy shopped at *Old Army!* If Cousin Leroy could find pants that fit his rather stout, stocky frame at *Old Army* then I was fairly certain I should have no problem finding a pair of cargos… but I did. As it turned out, *Old Army* did in fact sell "larger sizes." They just didn't sell them in their actual stores. Instead, "larger sizes" were an on-line only special order. That of course meant there would be no possible way to get them in time for the engagement party.

With my tail between my legs, I finally broke down and walked past the food court and into *Wholesale Plus* where I imagined I could at least get a new pair of comfort fit, pleated *Slacks* from the men's department. Sure they weren't as casual as cargo pants, but at least they were snappy and I figured one out of two wasn't that bad. However, the largest size in the men's department was a thirty eight, meaning I'd have to buy a pair from the Tall and Fat department… where the smallest size was a forty six, conveniently skipping over anything close to my size.

Since too small wasn't an option, I had to go with too big. Later, at home, Fee had to alter them and I had to wear them. After being hemmed to look like clown pants, pretty much any snappiness they could have had was thrown right out the window. So, that weekend at the engagement party, I wasn't snappy. I wasn't casual. I was just a "husky" guy in *Slacks*.

-True Story. ❧

APPARENTLY THE TAPE WAS IN THE VCR

One night, while flipping through channels, I landed on a show called *American Motors*. I had never seen it before, but I'd heard it was decent. Apparently it was about a family whose business was building custom motorcycles. It wasn't exactly anything I was terribly interested in watching, so since it was getting late, I tossed the remote control to my roommate and went to bed.

The next morning, as I was getting ready for work, D-Love popped his head in to my room to offer his thoughts on the show. "Hey, Mac, just thought I'd let you know that show, *American Motors,* was pretty good. You should check it out sometime."

Even though I had zero interest in watching a reality television show about building motorcycles, I humored him with a polite, "oh, ok. Maybe I'll watch it the next time it's on."

He then replied with an unexpected, "Actually I taped last night's episode. It's in the VCR in case you want to check it out sometime."

"Uh, ok. Sounds good. I, uh, I'll do that," I half heartedly promised.

"Cool. You're really gonna like it. It's really good. So anyhow, have a good day at work, man." He then gave a little wave and shut the door behind him only to open in a second later to add "just wanted to throw out a quick reminder that the tapes in the VCR, so you don't forget. Anyhow, yeah, so, uh, it's in there. Ok, later." Once again he gave a little wave and shut the door.

Though D-Love was geeking around like an obsessed little fan boy, I didn't put much thought into it. Normally when he discovered something new that he liked, he would tell me all about it and insist that I check it out, so I figured this situation was no different. But oh, how I was wrong.

Later that morning, while I was at work, I got an email from him in which he droned on and on incessantly about the greatness of the show. He went into great detail describing the various personas of each of the characters as well as outlining a blow-by-blow synopsis of the events on the previous night's episode.

Aside from just sending the ten page email, he also attached dozens of photos, audio and video clips, and links to web sites that contained information about the show to help convince me that it was worthwhile. However, when it was all said and done, I still just flat out wasn't interested in watching a show about some family that builds bikes.

When I finished reading the first rather lengthy email, I noticed that he had sent me another. The second email was to remind me that the tape was in the VCR if I wanted to watch it when I got home.

Just as I was finishing the second email, the phone began ringing. Since the only phone in our department of the library sits on one of my co-worker's desks, a solid fifty feet across the main reading room, I assumed she would answer it, therefore I paid little attention to it as I attempted to reply to D-Love's email. However, by the third ring, I could no longer ignore it. I looked across the room at her to see what exactly she was doing that prohibited her from answering the phone. As it turned out, she was hard at work, clipping her toe nails. Needless to say, at that point, it became clear that she had no intension of picking up the phone.

Grudgingly, I got up and walked across the room. I approached her desk and reached for the phone when she looked up at me with a smile and said "you smell like my boyfriend." Before I could offer a polite "thank you," a stray toe nail clipping shot me in the forehead, thus eliminating any civility I would have otherwise been inclined to use.

Dodging the shrapnel that flew from her feet, I finally answered the phone. "Library, this is Mac" I said as I watched another stray toe nail ricochet off of a near by lamp, landing on a table.

"Mac, sup? It's D." he said in a huff. "I just wanted to make sure you got that email and you know that I left the tape in the VCR for you." He continued huffing, then added "anyhow man, just figured I'd let you know that it's in there in case you want to check it out sometime. Alright man, talk to you later. Holla!"

Though slightly dumbfounded as to why D-Love was so adamant in requesting that I watch the show, I decided not to give it much thought, because my main focus was centered on the toe nail chunks that were whizzing by my head. But then, not even ten seconds later, the phone rang again. This time as soon as I picked up the phone, I could hear a voice ringing out.

"Dude, I forgot to tell you," D-Love began, this time in an even greater huff than before "the tape is already rewound so it's ready to go in case you want to check it out." He then took another moment to catch his breath. I tried to intervene and let him know that I really wasn't interested in watching the show. However, before I could get a word in, he began yammering on again. "You don't even have to rewind it. It's already taken care of. Anyhow man, I left the tape in the VCR in case you feel like checking it out." He then added "Holla!" and hung up immediately after.

At this point, I seriously began to worry. This sort of thing wasn't like D-Love at all. Up until then, not once had he ever called me at work, so it was a bit of a shock to receive two calls back to back. I couldn't help but wonder why he was so out of breath and why he was so obsessed with getting me this information. However, I couldn't think about it too much, because just moments after the previous call, he called back yet again.

"Oh my god, that feels good!" I could hear him scream as I picked the phone up off of the receiver.

"D? What's going on? What feels good?" I asked.

"Huh? Wha? Oh, Nothing, nothing. Listen, just to let you know, there are fresh batteries in the remote, so you're good to go.

Anyhow, man, the tape's in the VCR." Once again, before I could say anything, he ended the call with a very abrupt "holla!" and then hung up.

After putting the phone back on the receiver, I walked back over to my desk, where I proceeded to email D-Love to let him know that he could save his breath because I wasn't interested in watching the show. I was afraid that doing so would cause a back lash of emails and phone calls, but as it turned out, he never responded to the email, nor did he call back. Problem solved... or so I thought.

When I left work that afternoon, I was shocked to see a spray painted warning on the hood of my car, reading "Watch *American Motors,* or die!" On the side of the car, there was another message that had been keyed into the paint, reading "The tape is in the VCR."

As I drove home, infuriated, different scenarios of telling D-Love off raced through my mind. I couldn't wait to get home to give him a piece of my mind. I imagined myself kicking open the door and launching in to a tirade while I smacked him around and he cried like a little girl as he apologized. However, when the time came to unleash the tongue lashing I'd been mentally preparing during the car ride home, things didn't go as planned.

I flung the front door open and rather than shouting and screaming, I froze like a deer in head lights. I took a look around the room and was stunned to see that D-Love had redecorated the apartment with an *American Motors* theme. Pictures, posters, merchandise and memorabilia from the show were plastered all over the walls, floor and ceiling, covering every square inch of the living room. As the center piece of the combined living-dining area, D-Love had reconstructed Da Vinci's "Last Supper" at our kitchen table, using life sized wax replicas of the characters from the show. It was like something out of *The Twilight Zone.*

Rather than just leaving and never turning back, because I was familiar with horror film clichés, I knew I had to throw logic aside and further investigate the scene. As I walked down the hallway, which was covered with literally thousands of hand drawn sketches of D-Love's own custom motorcycles, I could have sworn

I heard a faint noise coming from his room. I crept up and pressed my ear to the door, listening more closely than I'd ever tried to listen to anything before. I heard nothing. It was strange. One second it was there, then the next there was nothing. So, being as irrational as possible, I decided to get even nosier and take a look inside. As I ever so slowly began turning the door knob, I was jolted by the sound of D-Love's voice in my ear, asking "Hey, Mac, whatcha' doin'?"

"Bah!" I screamed, to keep in accordance to horror film cliché standard reactions, as I threw my hands up and contorted my face into an exaggerated expression of surprise. "Whew, you, uh, you snuck up on me, there," I said, stating the obvious, since he had just snuck up on me.

"Whatcha' doin'?" D-Love asked politely.

"Uh, nothing. I, uh, just wanted to tell you that I like the way you redecorated the apartment." I most cowardly responded.

"Oh, yeah, thanks. I picked up a few new things today. You don't think it's too much do you?" he asked, oblivious to the insanity that surrounded him.

"Um, no, it's not too much. I, uh, I just think…" I stopped for a second, after noticing what looked like blood on D-Love's shirt. "Uh, D, what's that on your shirt?" I enquired.

"This? Oh, it's just a little blood from my tattoo," he said, as he began lifting his shirt. "What do you think?" he asked as he revealed the *American Motors* logo that was carved into his chest. "I did it myself. It hurt like hell, but I think it was worth it," he explained.

Completely dumbfounded, I was left standing there, with no verbal response, just shaking my head with my mouth open in awe. After a few moments, D-Love tucked his shirt back in and said "Hey, I don't remember if I told you or not, but I taped it and it's in the VCR if you want to check it out."

"Yeah, D, you told me. You even spray painted it on my car." I boldly reminded him.

"What? That wasn't me," he denied. "That could have been anyone," he then suggested.

"D, there's a picture of you spraying my car, hanging in our living room," I said as I pointed to the picture of D-Love spray painting my car that was hanging in our living room.

"That's someone else's red 1977 Chevy Camaro. It's a popular car, Mac." D-Love argued then added, "Are you calling me a liar? I don't like being called a liar, Mac," he asserted as he twitched and scratched at his chest. He then pulled a magic marker from his pocket and began waving it in front of my face. "Listen here, Mac, I've been nice but I'm done with that. Now we're going into the living room and you're going to sit down and watch the show that I taped and left in the VCR for you. And you'll do it right now or there's gonna be some magic marker mustache mayhem all night up in here!"

Finally out of fear for my own well being, I sat down and watched the tape of *American Motors* that D-Love had left in the VCR. At first I couldn't focus the tape, so I kept adjusting the tracking until I realized he had taped the show with a cam-corder. For the life of me I couldn't figure out why, but D-Love had actually bootlegged a television show. I asked him why and he explained that something about the shaky, out of focus camera shots made it "dirtier and sexier."

So I watched the show and to be kind, it was crap. Basically a family of bike builders sit around and bicker with each other while they feebly attempt to build motorcycles. It was just a mediocre show and there was nothing special about it to warrant the freakish obsession D-Love had created in that crazy little head of his. As the credits rolled, D-Love asked me what I thought of the show.

"It was ok," I said.

"Ok? OK! What do you mean ok? It was the best show ever!" D-Love asserted.

"Well...ok...it was good then," I offered as to not hurt his feelings or further enrage him. However, rather than yelling or threatening my life, he responded in a way I had never seen in any horror film, so it was unexpected to say the least.

"You're only saying that because that's what I want to hear. If you didn't like it, you could have said so," he retorted as he began to tear up like a woman whose feelings had just been hurt. Then out of pity, I tried to console him. "...it was good. Really....really it was..." I tried to convince him as I rubbed his shoulders. Then, upon realizing just how gay that actually seemed, I quickly pulled my hands away. Just then he started yelling again.

"That's right, don't touch me! You're a liar and I hate you!" he shrieked as he got off the couch. He ran towards his room and turned back to once again scream "I hate you!" then he slammed his door. Even though I couldn't see it, I was almost positive that he stood on the other side of the door, muttering in a barely audible whisper, "I hate you....I hate you..." as he sobbed uncontrollably. He then locked the door and stayed in his room for the rest of the night.

The next morning, I awoke to the sound of D-Love knocking on my door. I answered the door and he popped his head in to apologize. "Hey, Mac, sorry if I acted a little crazy yesterday but I just really liked the show, and I thought you would too. But I guess you're right. It's not that great of a show, so I got rid of all of the *American Motors* stuff in the apartment and everything is back to normal. Anyhow, man, have a good day at work." He then waved and shut the door behind him. A second later, he then re-opened the door and popped his head in again. "Oh, I almost forgot, I saw that show *Pimp My Wheels* last night. It was pretty good. I taped last night's episode if you want to check it out. It's in the VCR." He then waved and shut the door behind him.

-True Story. ❧

HOW I GOT FROSTBITE IN AUGUST

There are few things in life that I enjoy more than the simple pleasure of just laying on my couch and zoning out. I truly cherish the times when the frenzy of everyday life has come to a halt just long enough that I'm afforded a brief moment to just sit around and do nothing at all. When I find myself wrapped in the blissful splendor of one of these moments, all of my stress melts away and I feel weightless, as if I'm floating up to my own personal heaven.

One Saturday afternoon I was in the midst of enjoying such a moment when I was interrupted by the intrusive sound of the telephone, blaring in my ear. As the ringing continued, I contemplated whether or not it would behoove me to answer the phone. I also put a considerable amount of thought into whether or not I'd ever find a way to work the phrase "behoove me" into a sentence. Ultimately, I came up with nothing and decided to answer the phone after realizing I hadn't remembered to turn on the answering machine.

Disgusted as I was that my moment of Zen was interrupted, I still managed to be as cordial as possible to whomever it was awaiting me on the other line. "What!" I offered as the friendliest greeting I could muster.

"Mac, sup? It's Leroy," he said, pausing to smack his lips as he was obviously eating a sandwich or some potato chips or toe nail clippings or whatever it was that Leroy happened to have handy. After a few obnoxious smacks, he continued, "Dude, look," only to pause again and commence with the lip smacking. After one final smack followed by a gulp, he continued "Dude, listen, man. I'm givin' my girlfriend my old couch, right. So can you help me move it over there?"

Desperately wanting to revert back to the blissful state of peace I had been in moments before, I was convinced that I could recapture that feeling if only I could dismiss my cousin and pretend I was never interrupted.

"Nah, Leroy, I'm busy. Maybe some other time, ok?" As soon as the words left my mouth, I held the phone out to locate the "Off" button, which I had every intention of pressing. However, the split second that it took to find the button left Leroy a window of opportunity to change my mind. He exploited that opportunity to it's fullest by taking me on a guilt trip.

"Busy? Oh, oh I see. I see how it is, cousin," I could here him say as my finger stayed poised above the "off" button. As the guilt began seeping into my conscience I put the phone back up to my ear to hear the rest of Leroy's plea.

"Sometimes I'm busy. I'm never too busy to help family, though. But maybe that's just me. I'm a nice guy like that. I help my family when they call. But whatever, man, that's cool. I'll just do it myself. It'll only take five minutes anyhow. But I guess you're too busy to help your own cousin for five whole minutes. Whatever, though. It's cool. You know, I'll just pretend like I don't even have a cousin. It's cool, don't worry about it. Don't worry about me having to move a couch all by myself. It's cool. Just don't worry about me pulling my back out or anything while I'm moving a couch all by myself because my cousin is too busy to help me. It's cool."

After about the fifth "it's cool," I grudgingly decided to help Leroy out for what he promised would be five minutes worth of work.

"Ok, I'll be there in a minute," I sighed. After hanging up the phone it became apparent that the brief moment of bliss before Leroy called would be as close as I was going to get to achieving personal enlightenment that Saturday.

When I pulled my Camaro up to Leroy's apartment, I was

immediately pissed that I forgot to bring my coat, scarf and mittens. Though it was August, without such survival gear, I knew I could easily run the risk of losing appendages to frostbite in that meat freezer he called an apartment. After a five minute visit to Leroy's you have to chisel ice off your zipper to go to the bathroom. It's that cold.

I sat outside his apartment contemplating whether or not I should turn back and get my thermal underwear for protection, when after about thirty seconds of mentally listing the pros and cons of driving back to my place, I ultimately decided to stay. "It'll only take a second. I'm moving a couch. How long can it take? . . . yeah, it'll only take a second."

As I walked into the frozen tundra that is Leroy's apartment, I was not only blown away by the powerful blasts of arctic air coming from his industrial strength air conditioner, I was also taken aback by the fact that he was sitting on the very same couch I was to help him move. Not only was he sitting on the couch, but he was eating a ham salad sandwich, and getting crumbs everywhere. That in and of itself didn't bother me, but rather it was what else was on the couch that struck a cord. Along side him were large piles of clothing, books, and various tools, powered and otherwise.

"What's with all the crap on your couch?" I asked.

"What? . . . oh, this stuff? Yeah, we gotta move that before we pick up the couch," he said as he picked ham salad from between his teeth and made a loud sucking sound.

I was absolutely ecstatic to be informed that "we" would be moving Leroy's junk pile. As excited as I was, I still somehow mustered the willpower to keep my whimsical glee to a minimum as I stood patiently awaiting a signal that "we" were ready to move the massive heap of Leroy's belongings off the couch. As it turned out, no signal would be given for quite some time.

"Are we gonna move this stuff so we can move the couch?" I asked while shivering.

Leroy took the last bite of his ham salad sandwich and began picking his teeth yet again.

"Dude" He began just before sucking his teeth for what had

to be the millionth time. He then held out his plate, adding "make me another sandwich so I can catch the end of this movie."

"Are you out of your damned mind?" I yelled . . . in my mind. In reality I made him another sandwich.

"What the hell is this?" Leroy asked as I handed him his sandwich.

"It's ham salad," I returned.

"Uh . . . the crust?" he said as he held up the sandwich, pointing to the crust I had forgotten to trim from the bread. I took his sandwich from him and smashed it in his face...once again, in my mind. But in reality, I took it to the kitchen and cut off the crust then went back into the living room to give him his crust free ham salad sandwich.

"Happy now?" I asked as I continued to shiver.

"Dude, be quite. There's only like an hour and a half left in this movie and I don't want to miss it." Leroy said as he began devouring the sandwich.

Four sandwiches and an hour and half later, "we" finished watching some straight to DVD action flick. I think the movie was called *The Extreme Extremist 2: Extremely Extreme* or something to that effect. So with the movie over, it was finally time to move the couch, which was a good thing, because I needed to move around and help circulate the blood in my veins which was slowly turning into ice.

As I began tossing various articles of clothing here and there to get them off of the couch, Leroy interrupted me. "Dude, I gotta do laundry real quick."

Bewildered, I turned and asked a very apt "why?"

"'Cuz I gotta do the clothes that are in my hamper now, so I can put these clothes in the hamper when those are done" he said, oblivious to the irrationality of his explanation.

Rather than fighting it, I just caved in and decided waiting for Leroy to do his laundry couldn't be that bad. While Leroy began his laundry, I shuffled my feet and rubbed my arms frantically trying to keep warm. As I stood there, blowing my warm breath into my hands to keep frost bite from setting in, Leroy walked back in from the laundry room with a defeated look in his eye, as if the task of doing laundry had defeated him.

"I need some detergent," he confessed.

I agreed to take Leroy to the store for laundry detergent, only because I was anxious to get out of the cold and feel the familiar warmth of sunlight on my face once again. So it was off to the store we went.

When we got back from the store, and Leroy had gotten his laundry finished and put away, it was finally time to move the couch...or so I thought. As it seemed, Leroy had several books on the couch, so of course he had to do some homework before he could put the books away. But he couldn't put the books away because there was no room on his book shelf, so "we" re-organized his book shelf to accommodate the new books that had previously resided on the couch.

Once that task was accomplished, "we" had the privilege of putting Leroy's tools into his utility closet. This also had to be re-organized, which was a real treat since "we" wanted to separate all of the loose nuts and bolts by size, color and material and place them into individual labeled containers. Of course that required going to *House Depot* to by the containers . . . and the nuts and bolts.

Once we were back from *House Depot,* it was getting dark and when it gets dark and the temperature drops outside, Leroy turns the air on full blast to get it extra frigid as he reminded me, "I like it real cold when I sleep, man . . . like, real cold."

When Leroy turned up the air, finally pushed to the limit, I asked if I could run home and grab my coat, to which Leroy replied "dude, it's only gonna take a second to move this couch. You'll be fine." With that mind set, it was finally time to move the couch. The joy I felt in my heart, knowing that the day was almost over, was enough to warm me back up. "All right, let's do it," I asserted. I was so eager to move the couch that I barely even cared that I hadn't felt my toes in over an hour.

But my enthusiasm was quickly cut short and the dull pain from frozen limbs set back in, when Leroy dropped yet another bomb on me.

"We're gonna have to move the coffee table and end tables to get the couch out. Oh and we're gonna have to move that lamp and re-hang that clock on a different wall, because I've been meaning to do that for a while."

A chill ran back down my spine as I once again submitted to Leroy's will and "we" moved the furniture to clear a path for the couch to be moved. Once the path was clear, "we" hoisted the couch and began inching it towards the door way. As "we" reached the door, it became obvious that the couch wouldn't fit through the opening unless the legs were removed. So "we" got out the tools, that "we" spent most of the afternoon putting away, and took the legs off the couch. Once free from obstructive protrusions, the couch was small enough to fit through the door way.

"Halle-freakin-lujah!" That's all I could think in my frozen little mind. "Hallelujah."

As we got the couch outside, it was then that my cousin Leroy asked me something I'll never forget. He looked at me with a straight face and asked " . . . Uh . . . so . . . what's the deal? . . . You, uh, you don't have a truck to put this in?"

Normally, I would have laughed at how desperate the situation had gotten. I really would have. But I just couldn't laugh because my mouth was frozen shut. So in silence, I waved goodbye to Leroy and went back home where I was finally able to lay back down on my couch and zone out, as I had intended to earlier in the day. Even though I finally regained feeling in my arms and legs, I did end up losing my pinky toe to frost bite while in Leroy's apartment. No big deal, though. It was just a pinky toe. I can live with that as long as I never move furniture for my cousin again.

-True Story. ࣱ

Some Assembly Required*

Once upon a time, I decided to buy a new computer. Being a complete sucker that was born yesterday, I decided to venture over to the local *Good Buy* where I eagerly anticipated being ripped off. "I'd like to be ripped off, please," I informed the salesman as I waltzed up to the desk. "I'm interested in overpaying for something that will be frustrating to use. If it's at all possible, I'd like a computer that requires hundreds of dollars worth of additional software and accessories in order to perform standard applications. Oh, and I'd also like an obscenely overpriced warranty that doesn't cover anything practical."

After giving the sales consultant the product specifications, he informed me that it was store policy to not actually have any items, that customers may actually request, readily available in stock. He then explained that he would, however, order my computer from the other *Good Buy* across town and that even though it was a mere fifteen minute drive, it would take four to six weeks for shipping. He also explained that there would be an exorbitant shipping cost as well as an additional special order fee. He was also gracious enough to set up a payment plan where I could pay forty percent interest. Being what my father always referred to as a "chooch," I felt this was reasonable and I had the sales consultant order my computer.

A few short months later, I picked up my brand new, yet already obsolete, computer and brought it home. When I got home,

I was shocked to see that my computer desk was sticking out of the top of the dumpster. I walked inside and demanded to know what was going on. "Fee, what happened to my desk?" I enquired.

"Pookie," she said she said with a laugh. "We're not keeping that desk your mom bought at a yard sale."

"What was wrong with it?" I asked defensively.

"That thing was a rickety piece of junk," Fee stated and then asked "True or false?" Rather than asking questions, Fee always made "true or false" statements. I have no idea why.

"Well, true, I guess. But it wasn't that bad," I admitted.

"Pookie," she began, "it was a makeshift desk constructed from particle board and PVC tubing. It was a piece of crap. And it would be nice to have a desk that isn't held together with duct tape. So I want you to go and get that cute little desk from *Bull's-eye* that's on sale."

"What? What desk at *Bull's-eye?*" I asked.

"The one I found the other day while I was scouting out the sales," she said as she rolled her eyes, signifying her disappointment in the fact that I wasn't up to speed with her latest wants and wishes. "I left a note by it, you'll see it," she explained.

Following Fee's instructions I went to *Bull's-eye* in search of a "cute" desk that had a note attached and sure enough I found it. I couldn't miss it. The bright neon pink sticky note with the words "Pookie, Buy this!" written in bold feminine handwriting was a dead give away.

Once I located the desk that Fee had scouted out, all I needed to do was find an employee to help me get it down from the top of the shelf, however, there were no employees to be found. This would have been pretty sweet had I been playing hide and seek, but since the desk I needed was in an enormous, heavy box at the top of a very tall shelf, I actually needed assistance. This meant that I had to wander around the store for a half an hour looking someone, anyone that could come to my aid. When I finally found someone in the lawn and garden section, I asked if they could call someone in furniture to assist me.

Rather than acknowledging my presence, the sales clerk just

leafed through a newspaper without giving off even the slightest signal that he even pretended to care. After a solid minute of ignoring me, he just got up and walked away without a word. He had somehow managed to take apathy towards customers to a whole new level that I didn't know was possible. Though miffed (yes, that's right, miffed) at his dispassionate attitude, I damn well respected his conviction.

At this point, I knew that if I wanted something done, I would have to do it myself. That being said, I paid some stupid kid, that I found playing video games in the electronics department, five bucks to climb up there and get it down for me. Although I was a bit nervous as I watched him nimbly climb the twenty foot tall metal shelf, I was also kind of excited at the possibility that he might fall and hurt himself. I never said I was a saint.

As he reached the top of the shelf, he began sliding the large box towards the ledge and it donned on me that someone would have to catch it or it would come crashing down to the ground. Well, actually, as I was jolted by the thunderous thud of the package smashing against the floor, followed by the sounds of wood splintering and miscellaneous metal pieces scattering across the tile, it dawned on me that we may need a better plan. But that's neither here nor there. The important thing was that as I contemplated a better means of getting the hefty package safely to the ground, I heard another thud. This time, the rubble from the first crash provided just enough cushioning to allow the second box to land safely.

Upon inspection of the package, I was pleased with its condition. I did however notice that the words "some assembly required" were written on the side. Of course, I quickly ignored the notice with a how-hard-could-it-be attitude. When I got home and opened the box, I realized that the phrase "some assembly required" was, to say the least, an understatement. If by "some assembly required" they meant "you must be proficient in astrophysics and Oni-Demon Magic to construct as shown," then yes, some assembly was required indeed.

Just trying to make heads or tails out of the individual components was a chore in and of itself. The kit came with the following materials: thirty four wing nuts, eighty five wood screws, a package of ten penny nails, one half of the fabled golden decoder amulet of the Gruun Temple, six brass knobs, nineteen flat head screws, one three ounce tube of glue, a few dozen vulcanized tungsten alloy staples, four blocks of wood, a lathe, four pressed particle boards, thirty feet of PVC tubing, one liter of weapons grade plutonium, the flux capacitor, and a one sixteenth inch Allen wrench, which apparently was the only tool necessary for the job.

There was an eight hundred page instruction booklet that came complete with a study guide and an interactive CD-ROM companion disc titled *Building Your New Desk- Discovering Your Inner Self Through The Magical Journey Of A Lifetime.* Not to mention the instructions were in what I can only guess was ancient Sanskrit, so to translate them I had to find the other half of the golden decoder amulet. There were more than three thousand individual steps listed in the booklet, most of which I couldn't imagine being practical, such as step eight hundred forty three, which, when loosely translated, called for "drinking one cup of virgin blood then reciting a passage from the book of the dead."

Looking at the massive mound of materials in front of me, I knew that I was in way over my head but I was determined to assemble it on my own. After spending a few hours sorting through the materials, translating the instructions, and watching the tutorial video, I was just as lost as when I began. I was starting to get desperate for a helping hand.

Normally, I would have called on D-Love's expertise, but as fate would have it, he was out of town at a *Pokemon* tournament, which he later denied being a part of. . . but I saw the trophy, so I knew the truth. With D-Love out of town, my options were pretty limited. Though I should have known better, I decided to call Cousin Leroy. He assured me that he would come over to help as soon as he was done re-organizing his DVD collection by reverse alphabetical order.

Three hours later, Cousin Leroy showed up, dressed only in his boxer shorts, carrying a half eaten bag of *Crunchy Chips.*

"Leroy? What the hell?" I asked, pointing to his outfit, or

lack there of.

"What?" he asked aloofly as he shoveled a handful of *Crunchy Chips* into his mouth. "It's after three o'clock on Sunday" he explained as he chewed with his mouth open. "You know that's pants taking off time", he continued as crumbs flew in all directions. "And when it's P-T-O-T, it's P-T-O-T", he added as he picked bits of corn chips from his back teeth. "Three quarter naked Sunday doesn't stop just because I leave the house", he added after a large gulp.

"Leroy, you're not helping me build a desk while you're in your underwear" I asserted.

"Dude," he began as he inhaled another fistful of chips, "do you want some help or not?"

Leroy had driven a hard bargain but I knew that with out him my chances of putting the desk together were slim to none. With that in mind, I grudgingly decided to accept Leroy's assistance. However, before we could get started, Leroy needed a sandwich. We of course didn't have any ham salad, so that meant no sandwiches and no sandwiches meant no Leroy.

With Leroy out of the picture, I only had one last option. Well, actually, two options. I knew that I could have called Buttons, who was quite a carpenter and had a vast array of tools, but I wasn't in the mood to be knocked unconscious from one of his devastating head butts, so that essentially left the one last option. Fee was my only hope.

Once Fee signed on to the project, she decided the instructions were not really instructions, rather they were merely suggestions, so she discarded them and drew up her own plans. She then informed me that she would need some new materials. "Pookie, before I get started I'm going to need you to run out and pick up a few dozen feet of pink ribbon, a couple yards of white angora fabric, some *Sour Candies* and this really cute *Vera Barkley* purse that I saw on sale. I left you a note."

I was a bit confused as to why she needed such frilly materials to build a desk. But since she was a big fan of those "sensibly chic" decorating shows on the home channel, I imagined that she would be taking some tips that she'd picked up over the years of loyal viewing and using them. I could imagine that she would use the angora to cover the boards and the ribbon to trim the sides and perhaps even add some bows as accents on the corners as well as adding lace for texture and glitter for sparkle. But since I'd never seen any of those shows, that was just what my imagination, and my imagination alone, lead me to believe. However, I couldn't imagine what the purse or the sour candy would be used for.

When I returned with the new materials, Fee giddily snatched them from me and ran into the back room. Giggling like a school girl, she excitedly said "Ok, I'll be in the other room, but don't come in. I want to surprise you, ok?" She then shut the door behind her. I had no idea what she was doing in there, considering she left all of the parts to the desk behind, but I could hear her snickering with delight as she revved up her sewing machine.

My mind was racing, trying to figure out just what exactly she was working on in there. A million questions that needed answers were flying through my head. Why was she using her sewing machine? When did we get a sewing machine for that matter? What other appliances do we have that I don't know about? How could I not know we had a sewing machine? How could she be building a desk with only ribbon, fabric, a purse and some candy? Was she MacGyver? What ever happened to MacGyver?

As I was pondering MacGyver's fate, Fee opened the door and triumphantly stepped out, proudly displaying her accomplishment, and ultimately answering all of my questions... except the questions about MacGyver, of course. She stood before me, holding the *Vera Barkley* purse, which now was trimmed with angora and pink ribbon, in one hand and a half eaten bag of *Sour Candies* in the other. "Oh, my god! This is the cutest purse ever! True or false?" she asked as she popped a handful of *Sour Candies* into her mouth.

Completely befuddled, I just stood there with my mouth open for a full thirty seconds before I could manage to put my lips together and ask "What? What about the desk?"

To which she replied, "Pfft, Pookie, that thing's too complicated. Like I could put that thing together. Pfft, get real." She then ate another handful of *Sour Candies* and continued admiring the cutest purse ever.

Although I was happy to see that Fee had yet another new purse, I was still left with no desk and no help. I finally sucked it up and decided that yet again, if I wanted something done, I would have to do it myself. But this time I couldn't find any stupid neighboring kids willing to do my bidding for five dollars so I was completely on my own.

It was a grueling and daunting task but I tackled it full force. I worked all through the night, hammering, taping, measuring, cutting, sawing, gluing, screwing, bolting, soldering, welding, cursing, kicking, screaming, laughing, praying, crying, banging, fastening, anchoring, bonding, bracing, buttoning, and duct taping until the sun came up. As I applied the last strip of duct tape, the sun rose, causing bright beams of light to shine through the blinds, illuminating the living room and providing a heavenly glow around the newly assembled computer desk.

Beautiful, breathtaking, and poetic are words that I could never use to describe the junk heap that sat before me. It looked exactly like the rickety piece of crap that Fee had thrown in the trash the day before. Though I hated the sight of the desk, I wasn't willing to scrap it and start over again. After all, I had devoted my entire heart and soul to its construction. It was a part of me. I couldn't get rid of it.

Well, I couldn't find it in my heart to say goodbye to the desk that I had so lovingly crafted with my own two hands until I attempted to place the computer on it. Apparently the desk was too fragile to handle the unbearable weight of the two pound flat panel monitor, so it collapsed like a flimsy house of cards.

After contemplating whether or not it was worth fixing the broken desk, I ultimately decided to throw it out and buy a new one. However, I wanted something that was pre-assembled that promised "No assembly required." Since I was in the mood to be ripped off, I ventured out to *Good Buy*, where I'd heard they kept plenty of pre-assembled computer desks readily available in stock.

-True Story. ♋

I WENT TO THE
STATE FAIR ONCE . . . ONCE

When I was a kid my parents would never take me to the State Fair, no matter how many times I begged and pleaded. No matter how good I was or how many chores I did, I always got the shaft. As far as I could see, there was absolutely nothing I could do to convince my parents to take me to the fair. I tried everything . . . mowing the lawn, taking out the trash, cleaning the gutters, washing the cars, re-shingling the roof . . . nothing worked.

Even though there seemed to be nothing I could do to convince them to take me to the fair, I still desperately clung on to the hope that someday they would. One year, in particular, I got my hopes up when I overheard my parents having a conversation with my brother. I was just coming back inside after a full day of working in the yard when I heard my mom say something about the fair. Because I was a stupid, I assumed they were about to go and that I would be going with them too.

I was really excited about the possibility of going that year because I just knew in my heart that I would finally get a chance to play the new ring tossing game I'd heard so much about from other kids. Allegedly, the object of the game was to toss a ring onto an empty milk bottle. Though the game itself didn't sound too thrilling, the prize was incredible . . . a giant stuffed teddy bear.

I wanted one of those giant teddy bears more than anything because I'd never had any toys of my own. My brother had toys though. But I couldn't play with them. I could only look. I had to pay him part of my allowance just to look at them and wonder what it would be like to play with them. If I ever got too close to the glass of the display case for his *He-Man* figures, he'd hold me down and fart on my head while he shouted, "I have the power!" My brother was a nice guy.

I was tired of not having any of my own toys so when I overheard the conversation my family was having I ran straight into the living room where I begged my parent's to take me to the fair so that I could win that bear. My dad, of course, looked up from his golf match on TV and nonchalantly replied, "we just went to the fair while you were mowing the lawn. Trust me, you didn't miss anything."

"Don't tell him that!" my mother sneered. "Honey, your father's just teasing. We didn't go to the fair," she said in her most convincing motherly voice. She then smiled and flung her arms open wide to hug me. This of course caused the candy apple she'd been chomping on to fall into her lap, thus staining the brand new, "I Just Went to the South Carolina State Fair," t-shirt she was wearing.

"Spit fire!" she yelled as she looked down upon the stain on her shirt. My mom always yelled "spit fire" when she was frustrated . . . I have no idea why. She then ran to the laundry room to find her magic cure all for all of life's little messes- "the stain stick."

As she treated the sticky caramel stain, she tried her best to make me feel better about being left out of yet another family outing. To this day I can still hear her voice echoing through out the house from the laundry room as she said "ok, truth time . . . your father and I take your brother every year and leave you at home to mow the lawn. I know it seems unfair . . . mostly because it is . . . but we love your brother and when it comes to you . . . well . . . you know . . ."

Needless to say, I didn't go to the fair that year. I didn't go the year after that either. Nor did I go the year after that. . . or the year after that. Year after year, the trend of disappointment continued until finally my spirit was broken and I stopped caring about the fair all together. Once that happened, I decided that going to the fair was nothing I'd ever want to do, even if someone invited me to go with them. . . noone ever invited me.

By the time I was an adult, living on my own, I figured that my little boycott had gone on long enough and that perhaps I should give the fair a try, just to see if it was worth the hype. It was then that, for the first time in my life, I went to the South Carolina State Fair and holy crap, what a fantabulous freakin' time that was.

From the moment I arrived, the games began. First I got to play this fun game where I paid some toothless inbred hick ten dollars just so I could park my own car in a shoddy gravel parking lot a mile and half away from the fair entrance. I managed to park my car and not have my tires punctured by broken beer bottles that were lying about, so I guess I won that game.

Then the games continued when I got to the entrance gate. There I got to play another fun game called "wait in line for three hours." I waited for three hours and eighteen minutes, giving me the new high score. It was awesome!

Once I was inside the fair grounds, I was greeted by the stench of pig feces and corn dogs, as there were limitless "Ye Olde Corn Dog" stands and various barns, housing all sorts of animals, as far as the eye could see and nose could smell. Though the stench was wretched, everyone pretended like there was nothing wrong. A little girl up ahead of me was complaining about the smell, saying she was going to throw up, when her father, blue in the face from holding his breath, told her to stop crying because he didn't smell anything.

There were at least two hundred country fried rubes standing in line, sucking down foot long corn dogs while they waited to enter "the barn." Out of shear curiosity, I got in line so that I too could see what all the fuss was about. If that many people were willing to endure that foul of an odor, I could only imagine that something great was in that barn.

I liked to think that the Holy Grail or perhaps the Ark of the Covenant, or maybe even those glowing rocks from the second Indian Jones movie would have been in that barn, but no, they weren't. There was nothing cool in there at all, just prize winning pigs and cows that looked exactly like every other pig and cow I'd ever seen. However, since they were prize winners, I was supposed to feel slightly less ripped off.

As I exited the barn, I surveyed the fair grounds, hoping to find something of interest to merit the price of admission. As I scanned the crowd, I happened to notice my mom and dad standing in line for Elephant Ears along with my brother and his wife and daughter. The whole family was there, even cousin Leroy. I began waving at them from across the way, but they didn't notice me, so I began shouting, "hey, Ma! Ma!" at the top of my lungs, trying to get her attention.

My brother looked over his shoulder and saw me making my way through the crowd. He then snatched my niece up from the stroller and yelled "he's here! Run!" Then, leaving their Elephant Ears and other assorted goodies behind, they toppled over pedestrians as they fled the scene.

Rather than allowing feelings of abandonment to make me feel unwanted and worthless, I decided to it would be best to move on and not let anything affect my day. I figured I couldn't go wrong with riding the roller coasters, since they're just good old fashioned, heart pounding, adrenalin pumping, hundred mile an hour fun. But I was wrong as usual, since these rides were scary for all the wrong reasons. As far as I could imagine, I should have been scared by the speed, height, and number of loops on the roller coaster, not by the fact that I saw some crusty looking redneck, who favored Squirrel the Locksmith, duct taping a rail together minutes before I got on. Needless to say, riding the loop-de-loop was quite a religious experience.

After the roller coaster I was feeling a bit nauseous, so I thought it would be smart to eat something. I wanted to try some of the fair food I'd heard so much about. Not a day passes by without someone reminding me of how great fair food is, since you can only get it at the fair. And boy, were they right! At the fair, you can choose from such rare delicacies as "Ye Olde Corn Dogs," the fabled "Fiske Fries," or for the more cosmopolitan epicurean, they offered something completely unheard of to the western world, I believe they called it "Teriyaki Chicken."

Sluggish from exotic foods, the likes of which I'd never had,

I moseyed aimlessly through the fair grounds, looking for something of interest. Although bored out of my mind, I was however delighted to finally have a reason to mosey. Up until then I'd strolled, strutted, sauntered, shuffled, and even sashayed, but I had never moseyed, so that was nice.

Since having the opportunity to mosey around was the pinnacle of my experience at the fair, I was left with the desperate urge to make the adventure more worthwhile. I wondered around in search of something, anything that would enhance the quality of trip to the South Carolina State Fair for quite some time until I finally stumbled upon a gaming booth that offered the very same oversized stuffed teddy bears I had coveted so much in my youth as prizes. As soon as I saw it, I knew right away that I had to have it.

I eagerly approached the booth where a mullet toting, tobacco chewing redneck, donning a "wife beater" tank top, a Confederate Flag ball cap, tight jeans, an oversized belt buckle, and a name tag reading "Bubba Jr.," paused from thumbing through his book of southern stereotypes long enough to ask me, "You wanna try yer luck?"

I informed the nice toothless gentlemen that I had every intention of winning the giant teddy bear. "I'm going to win that bear," I confidently asserted as I threw five dollars on the counter.

"You cain't win that one," he said as he turned his head and spat out a thick brown glop of tobacco juice, most of which landed on his shoulder. As he wiped his shirt, he continued, "It's a dis-play." He then pointed to a lower shelf, filled with small trinkets and added, "butchya can win one-a them there *Bean Bag Dolls*."

"Listen up, Bubba, I didn't come here to win a *Bean Bag Doll*, I want the giant teddy bear." I demanded as I slid five dollars across the counter.

"Aight." Bubba Junior said as he handed me a ring.

He then gave me a tutorial as to how to play the game. Basically you had to toss a ring onto a bottle. It seemed simple enough but in all actuality it was the hardest game in the history of the world. It was absolutely impossible.

Every time I tossed a ring, there would be the same outcome: so close, yet so far. On countless occasions the ring would hit the top of the bottle, giving me false hope that it would land itself on the bottle's neck, but every single time, without fail, it would fall off at the last moment. Determined to win, I plunked down dollar after dollar, turn after turn. Several trips to the ATM and a few hundred dollars later, I had still gotten no where. I was no closer to winning after hours of tossing rings than I was on my first try. Even though I was feeling hopeless, I still decided to give it one last try.

"I'm giving it one more try," I told Bubba Junior, who stood next to me, cackling as he counted the money he'd just raked in. He then handed me one more ring. I took my time practicing the throw and mentally picturing the arc of projection that would be needed to hit the mark.

With intense focus, I drew back and tossed the ring. From the moment it left my finger tips, I knew it was a winner. It just felt right. I watched every second of its flight towards the bottles. With great anticipation, I held my breath as the ring hit the top of the bottle and began spinning around it. I could feel my heart pounding out of my chest with excitement. And just like that, the tables turned. The ring fell off to the side and once again I was a loser.

Completely crushed, feeling beaten and victimized, I did what anyone would do. I snatched that bear and ran like hell. I narrowly escaped the fair security guards, but I still got away clean and clear. Even though I'm pretty sure that I can never go back to the state fair without being arrested on sight, at least now, after long last, I finally have the giant teddy bear I always wanted. I can also now say that I went to the fair once . . . Once.

-True Story.

THE PANCAKE ODYSSEY

Early one Saturday morning, back when I lived with Buttons, I was standing in front of the refrigerator for a good half an hour, holding the door open and surveying its contents. I was hoping that the longer I stood there, the greater my chances would become in regards to finding something for breakfast that was at least moderately edible. However, rather than spotting anything that looked even remotely appetizing, I found a veritable cornucopia of Buttons' unidentifiable leftovers, including a fuzzy green thing, some orange sludge, a few mushy red things and a rather large amount of crunchy brown stuff.

As long as I'd lived with Buttons, he'd never thrown anything away; instead he just put it in the fridge as if it was a big Freon cooled trash can. Our fridge was a vast wasteland of forgotten and neglected moldy crap that, for some reason or another, Buttons just couldn't bear to part with. Whether it was the last bite of a sandwich, a tablespoon's worth of leftover pudding, a sip of soda, or an old shoe, it went in the fridge. And once it was in there, it stayed there for all of eternity where no one was allowed to throw it out.

No matter how outdated it was, if I threw it out, a scolding was sure to follow. I can remember on one particular occasion I threw out some Tupperware that contained what I assumed was a three month old, maggot infested, fuzzy slice of pizza. When Buttons came home and found it laying in the trash, he punched me in the kidney and yelled, "Ba-har! I was just about to drink that milk!"

"But it was solid and it was covered in mold and crawling with bacteria," I explained.

"I like to chew my milk! So what? Besides, only pansies eat fresh food!" He barked. "Real men eat bacteria for breakfast! It puts hair on your chest!" He said, as he ripped off his shirt. He then added a very definitive "I lift weights! Ba-har!" as he mule kicked me, sending me flying half way across the kitchen. That was the last time I ever dared throw anything of his away, no matter how disease ridden it appeared.

So, to avoid personal harm, I was careful that morning not to discard anything as I routed through expired condiments and spoiled dairy products. Just as I tossed aside something that could have either been peach cobbler or meat loaf, it dawned on me that no where in the junk pile we called a refrigerator would I ever find anything worth eating. So at that point, I decided it would be best to get dressed and go out for breakfast.

I wasn't in the mood for anything in particular, so I walked into the bedroom and asked Fee what she wanted. "Fee, I'm going out to pick up breakfast. What would you like to eat?"

She looked up from her *Modern Bride* magazine and aptly replied, "Pancakes would be good. True or false?"

"Pancakes, huh?" I asked, desperately hoping she would recognize the tone of indifference in my voice and change her mind.

"Pancakes," she repeated as she flipped through her magazine.

After having a second to think it over, I decided that having pancakes for breakfast wouldn't be so bad. They were nothing too terribly exciting, but they would do. After all, I was starting to get pretty hungry and when I'm hungry, I'm not very picky.

"Ok, I guess pancakes wouldn't be that bad. I'll be right back," I said as I grabbed my keys and headed for the door. By the time it took to walk out to my car, the thought of having pancakes began to grow on me. I'm sure that it was just because I was starving, but I actually started craving them. Ever since Fee suggested having pancakes, I couldn't get them off my mind. I needed them.

It had been a while since I'd been, but I could clearly remember there being two restaurants in town that specialized in serving pancakes. They both had very clever, cryptic names: *The Pancake House* and *The House of Pancakes*. Since *The House of Pancakes* was closer, it was the obvious first choice. However, as I drove into the parking lot, I found it was the wrong choice because at nine thirty in the morning, *The House of Pancakes* was complete anarchy.

I pulled my car up close enough to the building that I could get a look inside. I stared through the window and watched in awe as an angry mob swarmed the lobby and hoarded around the poor hostess who had that "deer caught in headlights" look on her face as she frantically attempted to schedule tables and hand out numbers. The crowd was so massive that it filled the lobby and spilled out into the street, where the line extended all the way down the block.

Directly outside the door, the truly dedicated pancake enthusiasts waited patiently in a makeshift tent village. Those who were just beyond the village were sleeping on the side walk; some in sleeping bags and others in chairs. A bit further down the line, the Red Cross was giving humanitarian aid to those so weary from standing, they were at the point of utter exhaustion. Further still, there was a rather hopeless looking bunch that just instinctively shuffled through the line like zombies with no motivation or sense of purpose.

In the middle of the line, a couple of geeks dressed as Darth Maul were trying to use "the power of the dark side" to escape police handcuffs as they were being escorted from the premises. Apparently, after learning that they had been waiting in the wrong line for *Episode I* tickets, things got ugly and they began attacking members of the crowd with their limited edition collectible replica light sabers.

And finally towards the end of the line, those who had just shown up were outraged to learn of the preposterous waiting period. Men were shouting, women were screaming, children were crying, dogs were barking, robots were break dancing. In the midst of the chaos, I spotted an old blind man who stood in silence, leaning against his cane. I rolled down my window to ask the old man how long I could expect to wait.

Without even raising his head, he began speaking in a deep, ominous voice. "To obtain what your heart truly desires, the wait is never too long. This is the path, young traveler. This is the path, indeed." Dramatically he then raised his head, revealing his hollow, colorless eyes, and totally creeping me out, as he added, "yea, for if you deviate from this path, you shall embark on a most arduous journey fraught with peril and laden with difficult obstacles. Despite your greatest efforts, even upon completion, your journey shall still be in vein. Yea, for you shall yield no reward if you stray from the path. This is the path. Do not stray from the path!" He then paused for a mere moment before shaking his finger, exclaiming, "Heed this warning, young traveler. Follow this path or suffer a fool's fate!" And then, in the blink of an eye, he vanished into thin air.

Now, if I heeded every warning given to me by some crazy old soothsayer, then I'd never get anything accomplished. More importantly, I'd starve to death. So, since I was hungry, I disregarded his prophecy and decided that rather than standing in line and waiting like a moron, it would be a lot easier to just drive twenty minutes across town to the *Pancake House*.

After unexpected heavy traffic turned a twenty minute drive into an hour drive, I, at long last, arrived at the Pancake House. Though I was ecstatic to finally get there, I was, however, a bit ruffled by one slight problem I noticed as I pulled into the parking lot. The *Pancake House* had apparently been bought out by *The Bagel Shop*. I walked into *The Bagel Shop* and used their phone to call Fee.

"Fee, listen," I began, "*The House of Pancakes* is packed out and the *Pancake House* isn't the even *Pancake House* anymore. Now it's *The Bagel Shop*. Do you just want a bagel or do you still need pancakes? Either way, I don't care. I'm just starving, so anything will do."

"Pookie, I want pancakes, so I guess you should just go to the *Pancake House* in Silver Street," she suggested. Being that Silver Street was another hour away combined with the fact that my Camaro only gets six miles to the gallon, I knew that I would have to stop for gas before venturing any further.

I pulled into the gas station to fill up my super sweet 1977 Chevy Camaro with premium grade gasoline, which I need for performance. I stepped out of the car and reached for the gas handle and to my surprise there was a rather sizeable grasshopper perched on the handle, starring right at me. I looked around and since there was absolutely no one in sight to witness me being a coward, I quickly swatted the icky bug away from me and gave myself a good overall shake down to make sure that the creature hadn't landed on me or flown into my ear to lay eggs that would eventually hatch, causing thousands of fully formed mutant grass-hoppers to burst out of my head and take over the world . . . I've heard it could happen.

As I began pumping gas, I tried shifting my thoughts away from being a pansy that was afraid of grasshoppers and focusing on something happy, like filling my belly with the fluffy golden good-ness of syrupy, buttery, heavenly pancakes. However, it was quite difficult to focus on any one thought in particular, due to the obnoxious Kenny G inspired Muzak that was blaring through the gas station's speaker system. Although it felt like my stomach was eating my spine, and my skin was crawling from the thought of a grasshopper flying into my ear, those irritations periled in compari-son to the torture of being subjected to a synthesized rendition of *By the Time This Night is Over* while pumping gas.

I had just begun cursing Kenny G under my breath when I glanced over to see yet another grasshopper perched on the pump beside me. At that moment, any ill thoughts regarding Kenny G, Muzak, saxophones, or synthesizers flew right out the window. All I could think about was that damned bug flying into my ear. I knew that if it did, then I would shriek like a little girl and anyone within ear shot would know that I was truly a wuss. Pride would not allow this to happen, so I clenched the gas handle tighter in hopes that for some illogical reason my grip would help compensate for the fact that I was afraid of a bug. Surprisingly, it didn't work.

As I pumped my gas, time stood still. I watched as each tick of the meter passed by as slowly as possible. The entire time, I kept my eyes on that meter, in hopes that the grasshopper wouldn't see me. I was under the impression they were like Raptors and if I didn't move, they wouldn't see me.

The time spent pumping gas was horrible. At one point I was pretty sure that the meter started going backwards just to torture me. Just as I finished putting the full five dollars worth into my tank, I quickly put the handle back in its place, trying my best to do so in one smooth motion that would allow me to pivot and turn away in time to avoid eye contact with the creature. Unfortunately my timing was off and I made eye contact with not only one but two of the critters. Then to my astonishment, I saw a third and a then a forth. They were everywhere.

I continued looking up the column of the gas pump until I could see the ceiling of the awning, where thousands of grasshoppers were hanging upside down like little eight legged bats. In the middle of the swarm, one giant grasshopper, who I assumed was the king, looked down at me and laughed . . . or chirped, it could go either way. Though I was initially paralyzed with the fear of a possible grasshopper attack, I mustered the courage to make a mad dash for the convenient store.

I ran across the parking lot, screaming and waving my arms until I reached the entrance. I flung open the door, jumped inside, slammed the door behind me and stood in front of it, bracing the door from the legion of grasshoppers that were sure to attempt to burst through at any moment. To my astonishment, no such onslaught followed. So, I took a deep breath and tried my best to relax. I then very calmly and collectively approached the cashier, who was staring at me like I was a moron.

"Lotta grasshoppers out there," I offered as an explanation for my stupidity. Rather than giving a verbal response, she just shook her head and took a drag off of her cigarette. I got the feeling that was her own special way of saying, "you're a moron."

I then paid her for the gas and headed toward the exit in shame. Rather than bravely walking out to my car in an attempt to hang on to my last remaining shred of dignity, I ran out screaming and crying like a coward. I'm not proud of it, but at least the flailing of my arms and sound of my screams scared the grasshoppers away long enough for me to get in the car and haul ass out of the parking lot.

I was still a little freaked out when I got to the *Pancake House* in Silver Street, but the simple fact that I made it there alive, was comforting enough for me. Not to mention I was also content with the fact that I was only mere moments away from ordering the biggest stack of pancakes I could get my hands on. The only downside was that I knew I'd have to wait until I got home to eat them because Fee would be upset if I ate pancakes without her.

In stark contrast to Columbia's *Pancake House,* the one in Silver Street was nearly desolate. There were two cars in the parking lot, besides my own. For a second I questioned whether or not they were open, but the big neon "Open" sign was a good omen. I wandered inside and walked up to the counter, where a man with an eye patch was placing his order.

"Hmm . . ." he began, "let me see," he then added before taking a long pause. "Well", he said before taking another pause to clear his throat. "What, uh, what's the story with these strawberry pancakes?" he asked.

"What do you mean?" asked the clerk.

"Well, are they just pancakes with strawberries on top or are the strawberries mixed in the batter?" he asked.

"The strawberries are on top," the clerk mumbled.

"Oh, I see," the one-eyed man responded. He then took a look at the menu and studied it closely. As he read over the menu, he kept looking up at the large menu board behind the counter with puzzled look on his face as if it had completely different information than the menu in his hand. After a few more minutes, he asked "so what's the deal with these blueberry pancakes? Are the blueberries on top or inside?"

"On top," the clerk impatiently answered with a huff.

"Oh, so they're all like that? Ok. I see," the one-eyed man said as he took yet another look at the menu. By this time even I had the menu memorized, and I had only looked at it twice, so I couldn't possibly understand why he needed to keep reading over the menu. Perhaps only having one eye somehow limited his ability to see that there were only four options; plain, strawberry, blueberry, and cherry. But that's neither here nor there. The fact was, there were four choices, yet the one eyed man still couldn't decide.

"Hmm . . . with the plain pancakes . . . those are just plain? I can't get syrup or butter?"

"You can get it on the side, sir," the clerk sighed.

"Oh, I see," replied the one-eyed man. He then took another look at the menu. After another fifteen minutes he finally asked about the cherry pancakes. He then took another ten minutes reading over the menu for what had to have been the millionth time. And it was then, that the clerk finally interjected. He reached across the counter, lowering the one-eyed man's menu, to look him directly in the eye, and asked "so what kind of pancakes would you like, sir?"

The one-eyed man then very aptly replied, "Oh, I'm not getting pancakes. I don't care for them at all. They don't agree me. So I'll just have a cup of coffee."

After the one eyed man finally got the hell out of the way, I ordered two large stacks of plain pancakes with extra butter and syrup on the side. I paid the clerk, got my pancakes and then raced home as fast as I could. The entire two hour drive was pure agony. Smelling those golden brown, fluffy pancakes while I was starving to death was pure torture, but nonetheless I endured.

Just as the sun was setting, at long last, I reached my apartment complex. Famished and exhausted, I flung open the door and stumbled inside. As I made my way to the kitchen, I yelled out to Fee that I was home with the pancakes. A moment later, as I was setting the table, Fee entered the room, donning quite a guilty look on her face.

"What is it, Fee?" I asked.

"Well, Pookie, um, I don't, uh, really want pancakes anymore," she admitted.

If it hadn't been for the fact that I was completely drained of every single ounce of energy in my body, I may have gotten upset by the fact that Fee had no desire to actually eat the pancakes she'd sent me half-way around the world to find. However, my spirit was broken and all I could do was stand there and listen to the sound of

Fee's voice as she continued speaking. "Ever since you mentioned *The Bagel Shop,* I've been craving bagels," she continued. "So can you run to *The Bagel Shop* and get me an un-toasted everything bagel with cream cheese on the side?" she asked.

I didn't argue and I didn't complain. I just threw my pancakes into the fridge and ran out to *The Bagel Shop* like the hero that I am. An hour and a half later, I triumphantly returned with Fee's everything bagel un-toasted with cream cheese on the side as she'd specified. Now that Fee was happy, I could finally eat my damned pancakes.

Utterly fatigued from my long journey, I moped into the kitchen and opened the refrigerator, where I stood there, leaning against the door, as I glanced at the shelves, hoping to spot my pancakes. Initially I didn't spot them among the barrage of random crap in our fridge, so I began rummaging through Button's old leftovers, hoping that perhaps it had just been moved and that I would find it buried under one of the various piles of mushy red things. Just as I was tossing aside some crunchy brown stuff, I was knocked to the ground by a swift kick to the rib cage.

"Ba-Har! What's up, fat ass!" Buttons yelled.

As I coughed up a small amount of blood, I looked up at Buttons and enquired as to the whereabouts of my pancakes. "Buttons, have you seen my pancakes?"

"Pancakes? You mean the ones you put in the fridge earlier? Dude, they were old, so I threw 'em out." He said, pointing to the trash can then stopping to stare at his bicep. "Damn my arms are huge!" he shouted. As he exited the room he once again kicked me in the ribs and laughed, "Ba-Har!"

After I managed to catch my breath, I picked myself up off the floor and once again found myself standing in front of the refrigerator, holding the door open and surveying its contents. I kept hoping that the longer I stood there, the greater my chances would become in regards to finding something edible.

-True Story.

YET ANOTHER DISAPPOINTING BIRTHDAY

Over the past twenty five years, I'd grown quite accustomed to being disappointed on my birthday. Every year had pretty much been the same; a "special" dinner at my parent's house followed by presents and "birthday cake." Even though my mom always tried to make the celebrations sound glamorous, surprisingly they weren't. The "special" dinner usually consisted of an entree I was deathly allergic to, yet my mom insisted was my favorite food. She would drone on and on about how she "specially" made it for my "special" day and it totally wasn't just something she happened to have been cooking without my interest in mind.

If the "special" dinners weren't enough to give me a warm and fuzzy feeling of love and acceptance, the presents generally did the trick. They were never wrapped in an effort to limit paper consumption and conserve natural resources, or so I was told. Regardless of wrapping, they were typically just re-gifted trinkets my mom received from her "secret pal" at work. As it stands, I have quite a collection of pencil sharpeners with my mom's name on them.

Though the celebrations were sub-par, to say the least, they were nowhere nearly as disastrous as the snafu that occurred on my fifth birthday. At least that's what I had to keep in mind each year as my mom presented the last remaining donut from a box of *Krispy Kreme's*, or a half eaten *Entenmann's* crumb cake, or something to that effect, and attempted to pawn it off as my "special" birthday cake.

My fifth birthday was a true monument to mortification. On that occasion I had three modest wishes. None of them came true. In my mind, my desires were nothing too improbable and being denied such humble requests made the ordeal somewhat of a bitter pill to swallow. After all, all I wanted was my own *He-Man* action figure, so that I wouldn't have to share with my brother, a party at *SuperFunWorld* and then, well, I wanted to be *He-Man*.

Looking back, I fully realize that my youthful disposition accounted for some of the letdowns I suffered that day. For instance, at the time, I figured that physically transforming into a cartoon hero was a practical gift my parents could have bestowed upon me, because, as I said, I was five. Though I later grew to understand that it was an impractical desire, at the time it was devastating to wake up on my birthday and find myself exactly as I was the night before; a husky kid sharing a room with his brother. That was just a tad bit disappointing in comparison to the fantasy I'd constructed in my head of waking up as *He-Man* and hanging out with *Battle Cat* in *Castle Grey Skull*.

Though in retrospect it was a bit silly to carry a heavy heart over something so foolish. The other reasons I felt disappointed on my fifth birthday seem quite reasonable. Instead of *He-Man,* I got the cheaply made Mexican knock off, *El-Hombre*. Though my mom insisted they were the same, *El-Hombre* was nothing like *He-Man*. In stark contrast to *He-Man's* blonde hair and blue eyes, *El-Hombre* donned black hair, black eyes, and a curly mustache.

Perhaps I could have overlooked the visual difference and played with it, that is, had its head and left leg not fallen off upon removing it from the package. I was a creative kid, but I just flat out lacked the imagination it took to pretend that a headless, legless Mexican was supposed to be *He-Man*. My dad of course remedied the situation in typical fashion; with duct tape. According to my dad, apparently, I was to imagine the duct tape was battle armor as if somehow that would make it suck less. It didn't.

In addition to the colossal *El-Hombre* letdown I was again heartbroken when, instead of having a *Super FunWorld* birthday party, like every other kid in school, I was treated to a substandard

Discount Town birthday party. Rather than being entertained by *Fun-zo the Clown,* juggling hamburgers and singing *Happy Birthday* to me in front of my jealous friends, I had the pleasure of hiding my face in embarrassment behind *Battle Armor El-Hombre* as my dad reminded everyone to order from the kid's menu and drink water. He did that, of course, as *Discount Town's* lame mascot, *Discount Dave,* stood in front of our table belting out the *Discount Town* theme song, which embarrassingly enough was set to the tune of the disco anthem "I Love the Nightlife." As *Discount Dave* did *The Hustle* and sang the ever so clever chorus, "I Love the nachos/I love the pizza/Here at *Discount Town,*" strangers stared, pointed, and laughed at us from across the restaurant.

After that truly magical experience at *Discount Town,* I insisted on never having another birthday party with my family in public ever again, hence the creation of the "special" dinner tradition. Though the "special" dinners left something to be desired, they kept me out of the public eye and that made them somewhat tolerable. Not to mention, they were all I had, so I had accept them. With that in mind, a few days before my twenty fifth birthday, I called my mom to check on what she had planned for the "special" dinner.

"Hey, Ma, it's me," I announced after a few seconds of listening to static on the other end of the line. I could visualize her on the other end, holding out the phone and squinting her eyes as she tried to look at the caller ID.

"Hello?" my mom finally asked after a tremendously long pause.

"Ma, it's me, Mac," I informed her. After yet another long pause, in which I can imagine she was still trying to check the caller ID, my mom yelled "Hello!" into the phone.

"Ma, it's me, Mac," I informed her again.

"Hello!" she yelled. "Hello! Hello!" my mom began shouting frantically on the other line. At this point, I knew she was beginning to panic. Her frenzied yelling could be the result of one thing and one thing only; she needed her glasses. After all, she needed them for everything, even non visual tasks like talking on the phone. "Hang on just a second! I can't find my glasses! You're gonna have to hang on!" She shrieked.

"Ma, you don't need your glasses to talk on the phone!" I reminded her.

"I can't find my glasses, you're going to have to talk to your father," she informed me as she put the phone down. In the background I could hear her yelling at my dad. "Get the phone while I look for my glasses!"

"Who is it?" I could hear my dad asking.

"Just get the phone while I look for my glasses!" My mom shouted. After another five minutes of bickering, my dad finally picked up the phone. Just before the sound of a dial tone cut him off, I could hear his muffled, distant sounding voice ask "How the hell do you work this thing? Am I supposed to press this bu..."

A few minutes later I called back. A few dozen rings after that, my dad finally answered the phone.

"Hello?" he asked before pressing several buttons on the key pad.

"Dad, listen, it's Mac. I just wanted to call to see what you had planned for . . ." I began only to be cut off by my dad, saying "hang on, your mother found her glasses. Talk to your mother." Somehow during the hand off, the phone was once again hung up.

On the third call, my mom finally had her glasses and somehow thanks to them, she was able to hear me.

"Ma, I just wanted to see what the plan was for the special dinner," I said.

"What special dinner?" my mom asked

"For my birthday," I explained.

After a momentary pause, followed by a sigh, my mom finally spoke, saying "right, happy birthday sweetie." She then added "just to let you know, I wasn't rolling my eyes or anything like that. I promise."

Not sure how to respond, I just said "Um, thanks," before adding, "But Ma, you know my birthday isn't until Thursday, right?"

"No, Thursday is family fun night, so that's not going to work, Mac," she very plainly stated as if it were a reminder of something I should have already known.

Bewildered, I asked, "Family fun night?"

"Spit fire!" my mom shouted. After another sigh, her voice took a gentle yet serious tone. "Ok, it's truth time. Every Thursday we take your brother out for family fun night. We never told you, because we didn't want you tagging along. It would just kinda ruin it if you were there. I'm sorry sweetie, but we can't just break those plans for your birthday."

Shocked, my mind scrabbled looking for the words to express how hurt and outraged I was to learn of my family's weekly outing that excluded me. However, the only thing I could manage to say was the desperate plea, "but, but it's my birthday."

"I know, but we just can't cancel our trip to *Super Fun World*," My mom explained.

"*Super Fun World?*" I asked.

"Spit fire! I did it again!" My mom yelled. She then added "uh, you're, uh, breaking up and I can't hear you" and then abruptly hung up the phone.

After taking a few minutes to bask in the warm glow of my mother's love, I came to the realization that finally, after long last, I was free from obligation to my family and that for the first time in my life, I could celebrate my birthday with my friends. I figured that for a milestone such as my twenty fifth birthday, I could be in store for something huge and since neither Fee nor D-Love had made any mention of throwing me a party, I assumed a surprise party was in the works.

In the days leading up to my impending surprise party, I dropped hints and attempted in round about ways to find out what they had in mind. Would it be a wild night on the town or a back yard party with a piñata? I was really hoping for the piñata. So I began asking questions, but my efforts were thwarted by Fee's uncanny ability to keep a secret.

Even up until the day before, Fee wouldn't crack. That night, as we were fixing our plates for dinner, I once again attempted to unveil the shroud of mystery that surrounded my surprise party. "So . . . tomorrow . . . kind of a big day, huh?" I never claimed to be too subtle.

"Yeah! Its the season finale of *Singing Idol!* True or false?" Fee excitedly answered. D-Love then chimed in with a very upbeat "True dat!" and reached across the table where the two exchanged their secret handshake and shouted the code word "Jibba Jabba!" Then, just like that, they went back to casually buttering their mashed potatoes. They were really good at keeping secrets.

The next morning, unlike every other birthday, I woke up feeling wonderful. I couldn't wait to go to work and be bombarded by birthday cards, floral arrangements, chocolate assortments and cheer from co-workers. Not to mention, I couldn't wait for my birthday cake. At the library I work in they always make a huge deal out of everyone's birthday, so I was looking forward to it being my turn. I was also feeling quite chipper with a little extra pep in my step because I was looking forward to my surprise party. I was giddy all morning . . . until I got to work.

When I got to work that morning, as it would happen, there were no massive floral arrangements, no chocolate assortments, no cards, and no cheer awaiting my arrival. Instead I was greeted by grumpy co-workers and stacks of paperwork. Since I didn't even get so much as a "happy birthday," it wasn't much of a surprise that there was no cake that afternoon. Disappointing as it was, I still made it through the long work day, punched out, and headed home, filled with whimsical wonder of what may have been awaiting my arrival.

When I walked into the apartment, rather than being overcome by boisterous applause and shouts of birthday greetings from my friends, I found Fee and D-love sitting on the couch, wearing matching airbrushed "best friends forever" t-shirts, as they munched pop-corn and eagerly anticipated the season finale of *Singing Idol* to appear on television. I couldn't believe how cool they were playing the situation. They honestly had me thinking that they had forgotten my birthday and they were, in all actuality, only interested in watching *Singing Idol.*

"So . . . Whatcha doin'?" I nonchalantly asked as I placed my keys on the hook next to the door and glanced into the kitchen, trying to get a glimpse of my birthday cake and whatever other goodies they had cleverly stashed away.

"Pookie," Fee began in a serious tone, "the countdown to *Idol* has already started, so we're gonna need you to go into the other room so we can focus."

"It's go time!" D-Love shouted. Then, in unison, they shouted "Jibba Jabba!" and did their secret handshake. Though they tried their best to keep the secret, it was evident to me that the big surprise was waiting in the den. Why else would they have told me to go into the other room? Well, upon finding the den completely devoid of decorations, piñatas, cake, ice cream, or people, I realized that they told me to go into the other room because they were, in all actuality, only interested in watching *Singing Idol* and they wanted me out of the way.

Though I was utterly crushed to find that my best friend and roommate D-Love, as well as my loving fiancée, had both forgotten my birthday, I didn't have much time to dwell on the issue due to the fact that phone began ringing moments after entering the den.

"Yeah," I dispiritedly muttered into the receiver.

"What's up fat ass?" a loud voice barked on the other end.

"Hey, Buttons, what's up?" I sighed.

"Ba-Har! Tell Fee that we can't make it to the *Idol* party cuz' I had to take Bull to the hospital." Upon hearing the word "hospital" I snapped out of my depressive funk.

"Hospital? Is everything ok?" I enquired.

"Yeah, everything's fine. I had to take Bull because he started whining like a little pansy when his pansy little nose shattered and started spewing blood everywhere after I lightly gave him a light head butt," Buttons explained. He then added "Dude, he's a pansy. You know how he is."

"Oh, well, is he ok?" I asked.

"No, he's not ok. He's a pansy. That can't be cured, Mac," Buttons replied.

"I mean the nose. Is his nose ok?" I clarified.

"Oh, yeah, the nose is gonna be fine, but he's still a pansy, unlike me." He then paused before adding, "Ba-Har! I can bench press crazy amounts of weight!" As Buttons began barking and howling on the other end of the phone, I could hear the door bell ringing in the distance. I then heard D-Love shout "Mac, get the door!"

"I'm on the phone!" I defiantly yelled.

"The *Idol* countdown has begun and it shall not be interrupted! If I have to answer that door, so help me, I'll draw a mustache you won't soon forget! Now, get the door!" D-Love demanded. I then got off the phone with Buttons and walked into the other room, past the best friends forever, to answer the door. When I opened it, Cousin Leroy was on the other side, holding a bag of *Crunchy Chips* under one arm and what looked like it could have possibly been a birthday present under the other.

While he stood before me, inhaling *Crunchy Chips*, my eyes were fixated on the package under his right arm. As he went through his regular "dude, check it, they're the good kind" routine, I couldn't help but tune him out and draw all of my focus on the enigmatic package he was carrying. As he rambled on about how he hoped he wasn't too late for the *Singing Idol* finale all I could do was stare at the package and wonder. Could it actually be a gift? Is Cousin Leroy actually capable of such a gesture? Is he the only one who remembered my birthday? What could be in the box?

Though I was so enthralled with the mysterious package that I was completely lost in thought, I snapped back to reality when Leroy handed it to me. "Dude," he began smacking his lips, "this is for you." Not knowing what to do, I just stood there with a blank look on my face and held the package in my arms.

"Dude, open it already so I can watch *Idol*," Leroy instructed.

"The countdown has begun!" D-Love shouted in the background. Then, all together, Leroy, Fee, and D-Love shouted "Jibba! Jabba!"

Though I was curious as to what exactly "Jibba! Jabba!" meant and why I was the only one who didn't know, I decided to forget about it and follow Leroy's instructions. So I ripped open the box like a kid at Christmas where I found something I would have never expected. Inside the box, was a vintage *He-Man* figure, still in its original package. Completely dumbfounded, I had to ask, "Leroy, how did you get this?"

"Dude," he began, "I bought the Dolph Lundgren *Master's of the Universe* DVD for like fifteen bucks on the internet and this came with it ... figured you'd like it. So there ya go."

For a moment I was speechless. I couldn't believe that Leroy of all people would do something so thoughtful and touching. "Leroy, this is the nicest thing that anyone has ever..." I began only to be cut off by Leroy as he shoveled a handful of chips into his mouth and informed me, with crumbs flying, "dude, I'm gonna need that fifteen bucks." And just like that, a wave of disappointment came crashing down around me and the moment was over.

After writing Cousin Leroy a check, I retreated back to my room. For the rest of the night, rather than celebrating the milestone of my twenty fifth birthday with my nearest and dearest friends, I sat alone in my room staring at a *He-Man* figure I'd inadvertently purchased for myself. As I said, I'd grown quite accustomed to being disappointed on my birthday.

-True Story. ❧

WORST CHRISTMAS EVER

On the night of Christmas Eve, 1985, my brother and I were inside the house playing a nice game of "shut up and be quiet" while my mom took a nap on the couch. In between the rhythmic sound of her snores, a bell could faintly be heard ringing in the distance. Upon realizing that it wasn't just the sound of the room shaking as a result of my mom sawing logs, my brother and I ran to the window where we pressed our ears to the glass with the high hopes of hearing the bell sound once more. We knew that if only we could hear it again, we would know whether or not it was Santa's sleigh.

We sat in silence awaiting another ring from the bell. We didn't breath. We didn't move. We didn't blink. Each second was like an eternity. As I sat on the floor with my brother's cleats digging into my back, to give him a higher position on the window, my mind raced with questions that I couldn't help but wonder. Was that a sleigh bell? Could it be Santa? Is he coming here? When will it ring again? Is it getting closer? Why does my mom snore so loud? What happened to the bell? Why hasn't it rung again? Why does my brother have to stand on my back? Why is he wearing baseball cleats in December, inside the house, no less?

As the frost on the window cooled my cheek and I began to lose consciousness from holding my breath, I was granted the answer to the most important question. As the sound of the bell once more resonated through the night air again, all doubts were relieved that the bell was, in fact, a sleigh bell. Santa was near!

After proof positive confirmation that Santa was on his way, my brother and I raced up the stairs where we brushed our teeth, put on our pajamas, said our prayers and hopped in bed like good little kiddies are supposed to do. When he got to our house, he'd surely find us sleeping like angels and reward our previous year's good behavior by filling our stockings with trinkets and placing all of the toys we could wish for under the tree.

As I laid in bed that night, I fell fast asleep with the comfort of knowing I had been good all year round and that I would get my Christmas wish. After all, I heard Santa's sleigh with my own ears. He was on his way. Not to mention that earlier in the week I visited Santa next to the *The Steak and Fry Shop* in the food court at the mall, where I personally informed him of my humble Christmas wish; that being the lowly gift of the *G.I. Joe USS FLAGG Aircraft Carrier.*

It wasn't too much for a boy to ask. It was nothing special. It was just a six foot long aircraft carrier that doubled as a base of operations with enough room to house every single *G.I. Joe* figure ever made, as well as their vehicles ,weapons and gear. Of course, for me that didn't much. For me, it would have just basically served as *El-Hombre's* boat, but that's neither here nor there. The important thing was that it was the greatest toy ever invented in the history of toys . . . ever. It was the tangible medium for the abstract concept of happiness. And it was all I wanted. It would make me happy for the rest of my entire life.

He assured me I would have it. I even had the picture commemorating my diplomatic visit with Santa pinned to the fire place mantel to help jog his memory in case he had forgotten me by the time he made his way down to South Carolina. And with all of that in mind, there was no way I wouldn't get what I wanted. No way at all.

I was wrong.

I woke up Christmas morning and gave a big stretch and a hearty sigh of relief, knowing that lifelong happiness was mere moments away. Just as was tradition in our house, I ran into my parents' room to wake them so we could open Christmas presents, however I was a bit surprised when I found their room to be empty. Confused, I pulled back the covers on their bed…they weren't hiding there. I looked in their closet . . . nope, not there either. I opened the door to the bathroom . . . Nope, not there.

With not a trace of my parents to be found I got the feeling that they started Christmas without me. Then I glanced over to their alarm clock to see that it was twelve thirty in the afternoon and that I had overslept. I ran down the stairs in a flash and dashed into the living room where my spirit and dreams were shattered for the first, of many, many times during my childhood.

My parents were laying on the couch, still in their robes; my mom drinking coffee and my dad munching on fist full after fist full of pistachio nuts, while they watched my brother rip open gifts like the greedy little bastard that he is. I stood in the edge of the doorway, frozen in shock, as I watched my brother tear the wrapping paper off of box after box of *G.I. Joe, He-Man, Thunder Cats* and *Star Wars* toys which he would immediately discard by tossing to the side after saying "meh, what else did I get?"

"Wha . . . what's going on? You started without me?" I asked.

My mom looked up and, as she cooled her coffee by blowing into the mug, I was almost positive I remember hearing her mumble "oh, spit fire" before taking a sip. After her sip of coffee she looked up and cheerfully said "hey, baby, you're up!" with a big smile.

"Why didn't you wake me up?" I asked.

"Well . . . we didn't want to wake you up because . . . uh . . . we know you like to sleep late . . . plus . . . uh . . . ah hell, listen, we just wanted it to be special for us first before, well, you know . . . Before you came downstairs to join us," she explained.

Somehow her explanation was a bit less than comforting, however, at that moment, my spirits were still high. After all, I was just seconds away from receiving my gift from Santa and being happy forever.

I walked over to the tree and was taken aback by the sight of not one, but two, six foot long boxes towering before me. Could I have gotten two *G.I. Joe USS FLAGG Aircraft Carriers* to make my own fleet? That would have been even better and the fact that I overslept wouldn't even have mattered, because with two of them, I would never sleep again. I ran over to the first box and grabbed a corner of the paper and began peeling in back. As the paper tore, it exposed just a small bit of the box inside. I could see the lettering of the word "Craft…" on the side of the box. It was the happiest moment of my life.

"No, Mac, not that one. That one's for Mr. Perfect. The other one is yours," my mom instructed.

"Oh, we must have both gotten one," I thought to myself. "No big deal, I'll just unwrap the other one."

More than confident that I was getting a *G.I. Joe Aircraft Carrier,* I grabbed the corner of the wrapping paper and tore with full force. This time, as the paper ripped away from the box, a different kind of lettering was exposed, however the word "craft" was plain as day, so I was still excited, none the less. With one more final gigantic rip, all of the paper was torn away from the box and I could read what it had to say.

"Craft . . . sman . . . Craftsman . . . Craftsman, 6.5 hp 21 in. Deck Rear Bag Mower"

"Surprise! It's a lawn mower!" my mom said cheerfully.

"But I'm only five years old . . . what about my *G.I. Joes?*" I asked.

My dad, who was just about to eat another handful of pistachios, stopped short to answer me. "Your mother and I decided that it's about time you start pulling your weight around here, son. So when you get done cleaning up the mess your brother made with all of this wrapping paper, I'll take you outside, we'll put some gas in the new mower, then you can mow the lawn."

I didn't even have time to dispute my father before my brother made his presence known. "Out of the way, fat ass, you're standing in front of my last gift," he said, just before pushing me to the ground. He then stood on my back so that he could reach the top of the box.

"Don't stand on your brother's back," my mom scolded

"...without your cleats. They'll dig in to give you better balance," she added. "Mac, go get your brother's cleats out of the hall closet."

After getting my brother his cleats, he used me as a human ladder to reach the top of the package, which he unwrapped, starting from the top and working his way downward. For some reason, that allowed the best photo-opportunities, according to my mom. After un-wrapping his very own *G.I. Joe USS FLAGG,* my brother looked at it, looked at my parents, gave a shoulder shrug as he picked his nose, then once more said "meh, what else did I get?"

Later that afternoon, as I mowed the lawn, I couldn't help but wonder why Santa had gone back on his word. After all, he assured me that I would be getting everything I wanted for Christmas. As I emptied the mower's bag of grass clippings, my mom walked outside carrying a *G.I. Joe Air Craft Carrier* and right then I realized that it had all been a huge joke and that Santa did get me what I wanted and my parents were only teasing.

"Oh, this is the best Christmas ever! I knew Santa would grant my Christmas wish!" I shouted as my mom came closer.

"Santa's not real," my mom said as she changed direction and headed for the trash can, with what I could now plainly see was my brother's aircraft carrier . . . broken in half after ten minutes of abuse from brother. She then shut the lid to the trash can and walked away, back toward the house. Before closing the door, she yelled out one last holiday greeting.

"Hope you like the mower! You can do the back yard when you're done here! Merry Christmas!"

-True Story. ❧

Among Heroes and Giants

As I walked down the hallway to my boss's office, I was nearly floored by the overpowering aroma of, what I could only assume was, sweaty armpits and burnt cabbage. After a few moments of gasping for breath and dry heaving, I managed to pull myself back together. I then took a deep breath and decided to brave the stench by venturing into the office, where my boss, Trevor, was "diligently working," and by "diligently working," I mean surfing the internet while stuffing his face with the most putrid culinary concoction I'd ever seen. And yes, the smell was so horrific that I could actually see it fuming off of the plate in the form of a greenish-brown colored steam.

"Trevor?" I asked as I knocked on the door.

"I'm in the middle of important research!" he shrieked as he frantically closed out his internet applications. He then quickly swivelled his chair around and glanced up at me, giving a sigh of relief as he mumbled, "Oh, it's just you."

Still holding my breath and trying not to gag, I half heartedly offered a nonverbal greeting in the form of a head nod and fake smile.

"Well, do come in. It's so very nice to see you *ah-gain,*" he said pompously using the British pronunciation of the word "again" in an effort to sound sophisticated.

"Well, I hope you don't mind if I polish off the remaining portion of my lunch whilst we converse," Trevor added as he wiped some sort of gooey red sauce from his lips.

"No, I don't mind," I politely insisted despite the fact that the atrocious funk in the room was nearly bringing me to tears. "What exactly is it that you're eating?" I pretended to care out of politeness, as I nonchalantly covered my nose.

"Oh, this? It's just a little something I whipped up at home . . . curried goat liver with mango chutney and feta cheese crumbles on a bed of lentils and hummus." He paused to take another bite. "I found the recipe in *Pretentious Epicurean Monthly,* you know," he said condescendingly as he ostentatiously twirled his chopsticks before adding, "It's really quite delectable if I may say."

"Smells good," I replied as I fought back the urge to vomit.

"Oh, yes, it has a lovely bouquet," Trevor softly said as he wafted the greenish-brown steam towards his nostrils. After letting out a sigh of delight, he looked back at me and asked "so to what do I owe the pleasure of your visit?"

I was there to ask for a day off . . . not that I had any plans or that I needed it for any particular reason. I just felt it was long overdue since during my three year tenure as a lowly library technical assistant, being afforded the privilege of a day off was a nearly nonexistent occurrence. This of course was due to the fact that Isaac kept a "loose schedule," typically strolling in around ten and then hiding in his office until he left around noon for the day, subsequently requiring that "someone" stay behind and man the reference desk. Ninety nine times out of a hundred, because my coworkers also believed in Trevor's "loose schedule" philosophy, I was that "someone." As a result, I never once had an opportunity to take a day off.

So, not wanting to waste time, I took another quick breath and cut straight to the chase. "Listen, Trevor. I'd really like to take some time off, so . . .

"Ah, yes!" Trevor bellowed, cutting me off in mid sentence. "So, you're looking to ameliorate some of the cold harsh drudgery of your tedious profession with a day off, are you?" He mocked before cackling obnoxiously to celebrate the self-perceived comedic brilliance of his quip. In the middle of his self-congratulatory cackle-fest he began coughing uncontrollably, nearly choking. Then using his chopsticks to point to his plate, he swallowed, took a deep breath, and explained, "Whew! That's some spicy goat."

After clearing his throat again, he took another bite and continued, "Well, Mac, as you know, I've never *bean* one who believes in taking time off . . ."

"It's been! The word is been, not bean!" I shouted in my mind while covering my nose and waiting for the cackle that would signify he was joking, but it never came. Instead he droned on about the concept of "responsibility" and how "librarians have a duty to rotate their *shedule* around work." Since I was getting woozy from lack of oxygen, and irritated at his refusal to properly pronounce the word "schedule," I began tuning out most of what he was saying. All I can recall was something at the end of his lecture that went to the tune of, ". . . this one time, and this one time alone, I shall grant you the rest of the afternoon off. Thenceforth, spend your time wisely as it shall be the only day off you'll ever have."

After Trevor began cackling again, I excused myself from his office and ran down the hallway and up the stairs to my desk, where I could finally take a breath of fresh air. As soon as I reached into my top desk drawer for my car keys, the phone rang. Still trying to catch my breath, I answered the phone. "Library, this Mac."

"Mac, what's up, bud? It's Troy, you know, the Naughty Wizard." Troy the Naughty Wizard was one of Fee's friends. I had the pleasure of meeting him at our engagement party. According to Fee, Troy the Naughty Wizard was "the funniest guy in the world" and everything he did was "the funniest thing ever." But to me, he was the cool guy that got drunk and pants-ed me, in front of my friends, as well as a random group of strangers, at the engagement party. Needless to say, he wasn't my favorite person.

"Hey, Troy, what's up?" I sighed.

"Hey, Mac, I was just wondering, do you remember that time when I pulled your pants down in front of everyone?" he asked quite seriously. Before offering a sarcastic response, I hesitated for a moment and clung on to the hope that an apology was on its way and that perhaps, just maybe, he deserved another chance. "Cuz' that was the funniest thing ever!" Troy concluded, thus eliminating any possibility for redemption.

"Yeah, it was pretty funny," I said while rolling my eyes.

"Anyhow, man, I heard that you have the rest of the day off, so let's hang out!" Troy excitedly propositioned.

Bewildered as to how exactly that particular piece of information traveled so quickly, I enquired "how did you know that already?"

"Dude, D-Love sent me an email," Troy aptly replied.

"What? He sent you an email? I just found out about it, myself, two minutes ago. So how does D-Love already know?"

"Duh, D-Love knows everything," Troy answered. "So are we gonna hang out or what?"

Spending my first and probably last day off from work in three years with a grown man who called himself Troy the Naughty Wizard wasn't exactly high on my priority list. However, I knew that sacrificing my one and only day off to spend time with one of Fee's friends would be a gesture she would appreciate. So with that in mind, I grudgingly accepted Troy's invitation.

Since he was in the area, he offered to swing by and pick me up from work. A few minutes later, he came walking up to my desk with a disgusted look on his face, shouting, "Eew! It freaking reeks like sweaty armpits and burnt cabbage in here!"

His outburst, of course, caused everyone in the library stop and stare, first at him, then at me. At first I shook my head, pretending like I didn't know him, but that plan was shot down when he announced, "Seriously, Mac, my farts smell better than that!"

All I could do was bow my head in shame as Troy proceeded to lift his leg and pass gas, loud enough for all to hear, saying "See what I mean, Mac, old buddy? My farts do smell better. I mean seriously, Mac, take a whiff and tell me they don't smell better!"

Despite the utter humiliation I felt, my shame quickly turned to fear from the thought of Troy crossing paths with Trevor. I was afraid that Troy would do something juvenile that would, no doubt, get me fired so I grabbed Troy by the arm and began escorting him to the door. "Ok, good to see you Troy, let's get moving." I insisted.

"Aren't you going to introduce me to your co-workers?" Troy asked as I led him to the door.

"No time for that, we gotta run," I quickly answered.

As we made our way across the room, my heart was racing. I couldn't help but think that at any moment Trevor would pop up out of nowhere and I'd be forced to introduce him to Troy. And as luck would have it, five feet from the door, my entire world came to a screeching halt when Trevor, sure enough, popped out from nowhere.

My heart was pounding through my chest as he stood before me, adjusting his glasses with a perplexed look on his face. The tension was so thick it was almost palpable as I anxiously awaited Trevor's request for an introduction. My heart skipped a beat as he furrowed his brow in deep thought before asking, "Has someone been eating Tandoori Chicken?"

The feeling of relief for not having to introduce Trevor to Troy was overwhelming . . . so much so, that I didn't even answer his question. I just stood there with a stupid smile on my face until Trevor walked away, talking to himself, saying, "It smells wonderful in here."

"What was that all about?" Troy asked as we walked outside.

"Oh, it was nothing. Don't worry about it," I answered.

As Troy surveyed the parking lot, looking for his car, he reached into his pocket and grabbed his keys. After spotting his car, he nodded in its direction, and we began walking towards it. As we got in the car, I asked Troy what exactly he had planned. "So, what's the game plan? Where are we going?"

"It's a secret," Troy said with a giggle as he started the car. Without providing so much as a hint as to where we were going, Troy put the car in gear and took off down the road. As we drove for what seemed to be an eternity, I took a few stabs at making small talk with Troy, but every attempt went nowhere. All Troy wanted to talk about was how funny it was when he pulled my pants down in front of everyone. Needless to say, that wasn't exactly my favorite topic of conversation, so I kept my comments to a minimum.

After the most excruciating fifteen minutes I've ever spent riding in a car, we arrived at our destination. "This is it" Troy said, pointing to the large neon yellow sign that hung above the door, reading, *"Heroes and Giants Comic Book Shop."* A bit less than enthusiastic about spending my day off hanging out with a guy named Troy the Naughty Wizard in a comic shop, I asked "We're seriously going to hang out in a comic shop?"

"Dude, it's the most awesome place ever!" Troy asserted as he swung open the car door. Then in a flash, he hopped out of the car and ran giddily towards the entrance of *Heroes and Giants.* "Come on!" He yelled as he stood at the entrance, holding the door open. And with that, I got out of the car and walked up to the entrance of a comic book shop for the first time since I was twelve.

As we stood in the doorway, Troy threw his arm around my shoulder and asked "hey, you know what we used to do in high school?"

"What's that, Troy?" I asked.

He then answered by pulling my pants down and shoving me inside the comic book shop. While I pulled up my pants, Troy ran to the car, laughing like a mad man. As he peeled out of the parking lot, he yelled "see ya later, nerd!"

"Though Troy thought he was playing a cruel joke, it actually turned out being one of the best days of my life," I would like to be able to say when retelling this story. However, because Troy the Naughty Wizard pants-ed me in front of a bunch of comic book nerds, they all "felt my pain" and tried to befriend me, as I was "one of them." That said, I spent the entire rest of the afternoon, on my one and only day off from work, waiting on Fee to pick me up as I listened to my new "friends" flex their comic book knowledge and argue amongst themselves over which was the most powerful Thunder Cat. Apparently, it was Panthro.

-True Story. ॐ

ETHEL WENT TO LUNCH AT NOON

Cousin Leroy offered to take me out to lunch once. I thought he was joking at first, being that he'd never offered to pay for anything at all, ever, but it turned out he was for real. As it seemed, Cousin Leroy wanted to take me, and only me, out to some low rent Chinese dive called *Lo Fat Chen's* in order to celebrate my engagement to Fee. Sure it was a bit tacky that he neglected to invite my fiancée to a luncheon that was supposed to commemorate our engagement, explaining, "dude, I'm not the one marrying her, so I ain't payin' for her," and sure the prospect of moderately questionable buffet items from *Chen's* was nothing to get too terribly excited about, but despite all of that, I just couldn't bring myself to pass on the proposal. After all, dining on Cousin Leroy's dime was a once in a lifetime opportunity.

In order to take Leroy up on his most gracious offer, coordination of schedules was a must. After much deliberation it was determined that I would accommodate his schedule, which meant going to lunch at noon rather than my normally scheduled hour of one o'clock. This of course required switching lunch shifts with my elderly co-worker, Ethel, which I foolishly assumed wouldn't be too difficult of a task. After all, it was just switching lunch times.

In my mind, I imagined that all it would take to rearrange my schedule would be to walk up to her desk and say, "hey, Ethel, I'm meeting someone for lunch and I need to swap schedules with you today," and she would reply with either "ok," "sure, no problem," or perhaps even, "word to your mother, yo," as I suspected Ethel was a closet Vanilla Ice enthusiast.

However, little did I know, Ethel's entire perception of reality was constructed around one unwavering constant: the fact that she went to lunch at noon. Because she'd maintained the same precisely set work schedule for thirty some odd years, the mere suggestion of tampering with her routine was like smashing down the walls of her fragile little universe right in front of her.

"Ethel, I'm meeting someone for lunch, so I'm gonna need to switch..." I began.

"Switch? Switch?" Ethel asked frantically. The puzzled look on her face instantly turned to one of horror as she realized what was happening. She then winced back and gasped, "Oh, no. No! Not the lunches. This isn't about the lunches is it?"

Sensing things could get ugly, I shrugged my shoulders and tried to soften the blow as much as I could by smiling and meekly answering, "Uh, yeah, it's uh, it's about the lunches."

Obviously, my shoulder shrug-and-a-smile combo failed to soften the blow, since upon hearing the news, Ethel flinched as if having a heart attack. She then threw her hand up to her forehead and groaned, "Oh heaven help me."

As she began dizzily swaying back and forth, I tried to ease the situation, explaining, "uh yeah, see, I need you to switch with me. So I'll go at noon and, well, you know, you'll go at one."

In order to prevent a total collapse, she planted one hand on her desk, propping herself up. She then began panting heavily as she slowly inched her way toward her chair, using the edge of the desk as a safety rail.

"The world is crumbling around me," she mumbled as she slumped back into her seat.

Feeling guilty, I sympathetically attempted to explain the situation further, as if the actual explanation itself would somehow sooth her pain. "Ethel, I'm sorry to do this to you. I normally wouldn't have asked, except that..." I began.

She then raised her hand to cut me off in mid sentence.

"Just go," she whispered, "I'll be ok . . . I'll just be here . . . wasting away . . . starving to death until one o'clock." After a slight pause, she then sighed, "Just leave me be, so I that I may die in peace."

"Ethel, you're not going to die from waiting an extra hour to take lunch. It's only an hour," I explained, using my most compassionate voice.

"What? Who's there? I can't see anything," she said as she pulled out an afghan, that she happened to keep at her desk. She then draped the afghan over her shoulders, coughed and moaned, "it's so dark and so cold . . . oh, so very cold."

Not wanting Ethel's death on my conscience, I decided to suck it up and retract my request. I can recall saying something to the effect of, "Ethel, listen, I'll just cancel my plans. It's no big deal. We don't have to switch." But apparently I must not have said those words. No, obviously I must have said something much more powerful; enchanting even. Perhaps they were "magic words." Perhaps I may have unwittingly cast a spell . . . I didn't really know. Whatever the case may have been, my words contained so much cosmic power that they miraculously brought Ethel back from the very brink of death so that she could gleefully exclaim, "Oh, that would be super!" as she excitedly threw the afghan from her shoulders, jumped up from the chair and grabbed her purse, all in one fluid motion.

"Oh, before I go," she said before pausing to rummage through her purse, "just wanted to let you know that I'll be a little teeny tiny bit late coming back from lunch." She continued rummaging through her purse. "Got a few errands to run. You know how it is," she said as she triumphantly pulled her keys from the bottom of her purse. "But I should be back by three or so," she concluded.

"Three or so?" I asked.

"Well, yeah," she said with a roll of the eyes, "I need to run a few errands. These things take time, Mac."

"But I have to meet someone for lunch at noon." I explained.

"Well, can't you just call them and reschedule for three? I

mean, seriously, it's only a three hour difference. It's not like it's a big deal," she said, completely oblivious to the concept of irony. Before I could offer a retort of any kind, Ethel gave a quick wave, made a smooching sound and yelled "ciao!" as she headed out the door.

With Ethel gone for lunch I was stuck working the reference desk until she returned. Since I was left manning the fort, the way I saw it, I had three options for taking Leroy up on his lunch offer. I could either: call Cousin Leroy and ask him to reschedule, find someone to cover the desk, or just cancel and miss out on the opportunity of a lifetime.

Because Cousin Leroy was exceedingly cheap, but he refused to restrict himself to ordering only one item on any given menu, he was a buffet kind of guy. He lived for them. They were his passion. And since *Chen's* was his favorite and they only offered their "$3.99- All You Can Eat" buffet during lunch hours, I knew that my chances of convincing him to defer lunch to a later, menu-only, time were slim to none. Not to mention, he said, "dude, no," when I called him and asked him to consider postponement.

Since rescheduling was out of the question, I figured that perhaps my second option of getting someone to cover the desk was my next best bet. Because Cori was the closest co-worker to the reference desk, she was the obviously the first person I asked.

"Hey Cori?" I asked, getting her attention. "Can you cover the desk while I go to lunch?"

She looked up from filing her fingernails and took an extremely deep breath. "Ahhh… you smell like my boyfriend," she said.

"That's awesome, Cori. Really it is. But can you cover the desk?" I asked again.

"Oh, gee, Mac, I'm sorry, but I won't be able to do that for you," is what I imagined she must have meant when she rolled her eyes and huffed loudly before picking up where she left off filing her nails.

"Thanks, Cori," I mumbled as I turned in the direction of my boss's office. I walked down the hallway and into Trevor's office where he was sitting behind his desk, eating what looked and smelled like a bowl of dog food. In an effort to save time, I dispensed with the chit chat and didn't even ask what God awful concoction he was slurping up with his chopsticks. I just cut straight to the point, "Trevor, can you cover the desk for me while I go to lunch?"

Rather than answering with words, Trevor just belted out a high pitched cackle. Then he laughed and laughed and laughed until he lost control of himself and started crying. Though Trevor was being quite cryptic, I used my razor sharp intuitive skills to detect the subtle hint that he was unwilling to cover the desk, and I excused myself from his office.

At that point, I was out of options. The only other thing I could think of was to throw caution to the wind, abandon my post, and meet Leroy for lunch. That of course I just couldn't bring myself to do. After all, had I left my station for an hour, upwards of two, possibly even three, library patrons would have gone without service and I just wouldn't have been able to sleep at night knowing that I caused something like that to happen.

With that in mind, I had to suck it up and call Cousin Leroy back to decline the one and only offer he would ever make to buy me lunch. "Leroy, I'm really sorry, but I won't be able to meet you for lunch today."

"Dude, whatta ya mean you can't meet me for lunch?" Leroy asked.

"Well, Leroy, its simple," I explained. "Ethel went to lunch at noon."

-True Story. ✑

I Peaked at Twenty Five

I had an epiphany at work one day. I was just sitting at my desk as usual, making a difference in the world via cataloging periodicals, when it hit me; at the young age of twenty five, I'd peaked. Facing facts, I'd achieved more, professionally, than most library workers could hope to accomplish in a life time. In just three years, I had gone from lowly Library Technical Assistant to obtaining the most sought after position in the field: Library Technical Assistant II.

Clearly, the world was my oyster and I was a king among men, what with having the Roman numeral two added to my official title and all. However, despite my elevated status, I knew that my career had hit a brick wall. After all, I had reached the top, the pinnacle, the apex if you will, of my classification's pay grade. And in the bureaucratic state funded library system that meant there was nowhere to go, neither up nor down.

After taking a few hours to zone out at my desk and think things over, I came to the conclusion that the only way to secure future career advancement, without the danger of hitting another dead end, would be to seek out a vaguely described position for a large, privately funded, international multi-level conglomerate corporation. Then the best I could hope for would be a series of lateral promotions, through corporate re-structuring, re-classifying, re-shifting, and re-shuffling for the rest of my career, ensuring I never peak again.

Just as I came to this realization, as fate would have it, I got an unexpected phone call. "Mac, you have an unexpected phone call!" my coworker, Ethel, shouted as she hurled the phone at me from across the room . . . she had a tendency to inappropriately throw things, such as breakable electronic devices, but that's neither here nor there. Rather the important thing is that, due to Ethel's poor throwing ability, the phone dropped on the floor. Once again for clarity, it was definitely Ethel's poor throwing and not my catching that caused the phone to slip through my fingers and crack on the floor.

After picking up the slightly shattered and partially functioning phone, I answered it just as I always did; by singing the Library Song, "Thank you for calling the liiiibrar-y, the librar-y, the librar-y. Thank you for calling the liiiibrar-y, how may I be of assistance?"

"May I speak with Mac?" The woman on the other line asked.

"This is Mac." I answered in my normal voice, since I was only obligated to sing the one line.

"Hello, Mac. I'm a top level executive for the Large Privately Funded International Multi-level Conglomerate Corporation." She said before rhetorically asking "you know, LPFIMLCC?"

"I've heard of it," I needlessly lied.

Since my "knowledge" of her company had no bearing on the situation, she just continued without skipping a beat or bothering to call me out on my lie. "The reason I'm calling is in reference to your resume."

"My resume?" I asked.

"Yes, D-Love just emailed me your resume and after reviewing it, I've conveniently decided to interview you for a way too good to be true, vaguely described position with limitless possibilities for lateral advancement," she answered.

Thinking the offer sounded just a little too convenient and maybe even just a little too good to be true, I hesitated for a full three seconds before accepting it. "I'll take it! What time is the interview?"

"Well, you'll have to accommodate my schedule and meet at

my next earliest convenience because that will be more convenient for me," she explained.

"Ok, I have no problem accommodating your schedule. What would be most convenient for you?" I asked.

"Well, perhaps the most convenient time for me would be Tuesday at nine, because I have nothing else planned, so it's the most convenient time I can think of," she informed me. "Oh, and just for good measure, let me remind you once more that Tuesday at nine in the morning is convenient for me, so there's no reason I shouldn't be able to keep your appointment, since it's so convenient for me and all," she overstated for no apparent reason.

"Ok. See you there." I agreed before saying goodbye and hanging up the slightly shattered and partially functioning phone.

After that, nothing worth mentioning happened until that next Tuesday. Well... sure, there may have been a little "incident" in which Ethel blamed me for breaking the telephone. And then that "incident" may have escalated when Cori came to my defense... and sure Ethel may have even clocked Cori in the jaw several dozen times with a stapler just before an all out riot ensued. But like I said, nothing really worth mentioning happened.

Worth mentioning, however, was the fact that the very next Tuesday morning I went to the interview, bright and early, wearing my brand new brown belt which was far better than my old one because it perfectly matched my brown shoes. From what I'd been told, making sure your belt matches your shoes is the most important thing in the world.

When I walked in to the waiting room there were a few business types in suites just sitting around waiting, since that was sort of the whole general purpose of the room and all. Accepting the fact that I'd probably have to wait in the waiting room, I took a seat next to a rather nervous looking fellow in a blue blazer. "So what's everyone waiting for?" I whispered.

"What?" he nervously snapped.

"What's everyone waiting for?" I repeated.

Rather than answering, he just pointed his shaky finger at the receptionist... from hell. According to Nervous Guy, she was pure evil and she wouldn't call anyone's name. He told a rather graphic tale of some poor fool who dared to test her wrath. Apparently he made the mistake of speaking up for himself and demanding to know when his turn would come. Long story short, the receptionist from hell ate his soul. It was then that I realized it would be more appropriate to refer to Nervous Guy as Crazy Guy. Then I casually took another seat across the room.

After waiting for quite some time, I asked the receptionist when I could expect to be called. She looked up from her game of Solitaire and, upon cutting her eyes in my direction, her eyes lit up. "Oh, my god, your belt matches your shoes," she said apologetically. "I'm so sorry. If I would have noticed it earlier, I wouldn't have ignored you like I've been ignoring the rest of these losers."

"Hey, don't beat yourself up over it. These things happen," I sympathized.

"I'm so sorry, sir. What can I do for you?" She asked.

"Well, my name is Mac and I'm here to meet with the Top Level Executive. I have an interview that she herself set up to best fit her own schedule, so there's no reason she shouldn't be here. It's at nine o'clock, by the way." I informed the receptionist.

"Oh, unfortunately she isn't here today because she's terribly unprofessional. You can meet with a junior executive though." The receptionist said as she pointed to a rather sleazy looking guy in a flashy silk suit, who just so happened to be walking by at that particular moment.

He then walked over towards me, slicked back his oily hair for that used car salesman look, stuck out his hand to expose his gaudy jewelry and presented himself, "Hello, I'm a scum bag." He may or may not have introduced himself as such, but it was something to that effect. "Come on back to my office," he then instructed.

We went back to his office and I took a seat in a rather uncomfortable plastic chair with a large crack running down the middle while he sat behind a big mahogany desk in a lavish leather recliner. "I'm better than you." He stated.

"Pardon?" I asked.

"In case you were wondering why your chair is so crappy... just thought I'd spell it out so there's no confusion." He said with a smirk as he pulled a string on the sleeve of his suit. "Oops," he said as he continued to pull the string, "it seems that I must have accidentally left the price tag on here." He then yanked the tag off the suit coat, reached across the desk and placed it in my hand as he whispered, "two grand...oh yeah, that's right."

He then sat back in his seat and propped his feet up on the desk. "So, Mac, tell me about yourself," he insisted.

"Well," I began before he cut me off.

"They're Italian in case you were wondering," he said referring to his shoes. He then waited for me to look impressed. After I gave an obligatory "ooh and ah" he continued listening to himself speak. "Actually, Mac, before you start, let me tell you a little something about me and how I work and what I do here."

He then took his feet off the desk and got a very serious look on his face. "Without me, this company would crumble. You know why?" He rhetorically asked. And then without giving me a chance to fake my concern with a lie, he answered himself. "Because I'm a mover. I'm a shaker. I make things happen. I'm the go to guy. I always deliver. I'm a problem solver. There's nothing I can't do around here."

"Oh, good," I replied. "I was almost afraid you wouldn't be able to conduct the interview, since you're just a Junior Executive and all."

His smarmy look of confidence turned to one of embarrassment as he fumbled around trying to pick his words carefully. "Oh, uh, no, I can't, uh, I can't do that . . . uh, I mean, I really do have tons of pull around here and I'm really important. But no I can't interview you," he confessed.

"So what can you do?" I asked.

"Uh, well, I guess I'll just take your resume and give it the Top Level Executive. However, she's terribly unprofessional so you'll probably never hear from her again," he answered.

"So this was a complete waste of time?" I asked.

"It certainly was," he answered. "But I'd still like to show you my Rolex. Look. It's real," he said as he pointed to his watch. At that point, from what I could tell, the interview was effectively over so I politely thanked him for his time and excused myself from his office.

And then nothing really worth mentioning happened until I got back to the Library and reflected on the day's lesson. Well, sure, I may have stumbled across a mysterious brief case that inadvertently lead to a series of misadventures including several exciting car chases and a shoot out with Korean drug lords in an abandoned warehouse, but that's neither here nor there. The important thing is that I learned a valuable lesson about sacrificing your dreams for… no… wait… I didn't learn a lesson at all. Instead I just zoned out at work and became comfortable with the fact that I professionally peaked at a young age.

-True Story.

Sunday Gravy on a Saturday Night

A while back, since everything seems to have happened a while back, Cousin Leroy called and asked me out to lunch. He said he was going to *The Fondue Pot*. Since I wasn't a yuppie moron that was willing to pay eighty dollars to dip little chunks of stale bread into melted cheese, I lied and told him I'd already eaten. He said that was ok. He just wanted someone to hang out with. Apparently he felt awkward eating in a restaurant by himself, as many people do, so I couldn't blame him for that.

When I decided to join Cousin Leroy at *The Fondue Pot* I was under the impression I was providing him with company and nothing else. As it turned out, I was providing him a free meal at the most expensive restaurant in town and nothing else. He didn't even try to hide it. When I showed up to meet him for lunch, he had already eaten and had the bill waiting on the table. The second I was seated, without even so much as a "Hello," he sucked his teeth and said "Dude, thanks for getting lunch. I'll getcha next time," as he slid the bill across the table.

My first thought was to punch him . . . hard. But I restrained myself and after taking a moment to think it over, I came to the conclusion that Leroy's actions weren't rude. No, instead they were a blessing in disguise. When I really thought about it, I realized that if I had eaten lunch with him then I would have ended up paying for both of us anyhow . . . so in a round about way I actually saved money. Not to mention, since I showed up at the end of his meal, I was spared from having to listen to him smack his lips and suck his teeth as he inhaled fondue. I was also spared from having to hearing him drone on and on endlessly about his latest DVD purchases . . . it was actually the best lunch I'd ever had with Cousin Leroy.

A few moments later, while I was busy shelling out ninety seven dollars and change for the perfect lunch with Cousin Leroy, he casually mentioned something about how nice it would be for Fee and I to have an engagement party. Naturally I assumed it would never happen. I also assumed that in the unlikely event that it ever did somehow magically happen that Cousin Leroy would be hosting it, since he was the one who brought it up in the first place.

A few weeks went by with not even the slightest mention of the proposed engagement party, so I assumed it was just another empty gesture that would never materialize. But things suddenly changed early one Saturday morning when I awoke from a deep sleep to answer a call from Cousin Leroy.

"Dude," he began in typical fashion, smacking his lips. It was almost two in the morning, so he was more than likely taking a break from playing video games to snack on a ham salad sandwich. "This pimento cheese is awesome," he said, proving me wrong. He then smacked his lips a few dozen more times before asking, "So what's the story with this engagement party tomorrow?"

Totally caught off guard, and still groggy from sleeping, all I could manage to respond with was gibberish. "Wuzahuh?"

"Dude, the engagement party," he repeated in an attempt to jar my memory. Once again I opted for gibberish, responding with, "Wuza-who?" as I rubbed my eyes and sighed with exhaustion.

"Remember when I bought you lunch the other day? I told you about it then," he replied with a smack of the lips. After hearing his lips smack together, I suddenly caught a second wind and regained the ability to speak in comprehendible sentences. "Leroy," I began before clearing my throat, "You only mentioned it once and haven't said anything since." Then I yawned, getting the last bit of sleepiness out of my system and asked, "So how would I know it was tomorrow?" But before he could answer, I added, "And, by the way, I bought lunch that day."

"Dude, who bought lunch isn't important," he replied

defensively. "What's important is that you really need to get moving on the whole engagement party thing."

"I need to get moving on it? Since when?" I asked.

"Uh, since it's your engagement party," Leroy said before sucking his teeth.

"I've never heard of anyone planning their own engagement party," I argued.

"Well, dude, when was I supposed to have time to plan it? I just got a new video game and I'm way too far into it to take time off to plan an engagement party," he replied.

"What? I'm not planning my own engagement party. That's just stupid," I bluntly stated.

"Fine," he said in a huff. "I'll do it. I'll call you back in a few and let you know what's up."

A few minutes later, Cousin Leroy called back and filled me in on the details of the engagement party. "Dude, here's the deal," he began, "D-Love just emailed the invitations to everyone. So check your email to get the specifics, but basically, everybody's gonna be at yer place around six. Dinner's gonna be around seven. That should give you plenty of time to make yer Sunday Gravy."

"What? I'm not making Sunday Gravy!" I snapped.

"Dude, all you gotta do is throw some sausage and some meatballs into a pot of marinara. What's the big deal?" Leroy asked nonchalantly.

Shocked at Leroy's oversimplification of my recipe, I defended myself saying, "It's a bit more complicated than that. First off, it's called Sunday Gravy for a reason. It's usually cooked on Sunday, when you can throw all of the left over sausage and meat from the week into the gravy. Not to mention, it takes all day to cook. Plus I don't have anything left over from the week. I don't have any tomato sauce . . . I don't have any Italian sausage . . . I don't have anything to make the meatballs . . . I don't have anything. That's the big deal."

"Well, sounds like you need to go to the store," he said before belching into the phone.

"Leroy," I said in my most serious tone of voice, "I'm not going to the store and I'm not making Sunday Gravy. It's not happening, so plan something else."

"Come on," Leroy pleaded.

"I'm not going to the store!" I repeated before hanging up the phone.

The next morning . . . well, technically it was later that morning . . . I went to the store. It wasn't out of guilt for hanging up on my cousin that I went to the store. No, it was because D-Love barged into my room at seven thirty in the morning demanding that I make Sunday Gravy for the engagement party that night. Not to mention, as soon as D-Love uttered the words "Sunday Gravy," Fee jumped up out of bed and excitedly shouted, "Sunday Gravy!"

She then made a several "yummy" sounds and added, "Pookie, Sunday Gravy would be perfect for the engagement party, true or false?"

I didn't want to break her heart and say no, especially after she broke into song, singing, "Sunday Gravy on a Saturday night, makes me feel alright," so I decided to suck it up and go to the store . . . for Fee's sake.

Because I was making Sunday Gravy I had to go to *The Posh Market* over on the yuppie side of town. Normally I stayed far away from *The Posh Market* but it was the only store that carried the brand of Italian sausage I needed for the gravy. Without that sausage it just wouldn't have been the same, so I was left with no other choice.

Pulling into the parking lot of *The Posh Market* was like driving into the heart of a gangland where a turf war was in full effect . . . Except it was way more frightening. It became obvious from the minute I drove into the parking lot that *The Posh Market* was run by private school soccer moms who didn't take kindly to the country club trophy wives who were invading their turf. So, in an effort to keep them out, they circled the parking lot in hordes, filling every available space with their luxury mini-vans.

As an outsider, I had to compete with the soccer moms, who were hell bent on keeping their turf, as well as the blood thirsty country club trophy wives that were determined to overtake the parking lot with their oversized luxury SUVs. The competition was fierce, but after circling the lot a few dozen times I finally lucked out and found a spot way in the back.

From the moment I stepped out of my Camaro, I felt uncomfortable. Soccer moms and trophy wives alike glared at me with contempt for taking one of their parking spaces and disrupting the balance of their fragile yuppie microcosm. With each step closer to the entrance, the looks became more and more hateful. One woman even turned her nose up at me as she said "hmmph," and walked away. Then in the distance, a woman in a black SUV rolled down her window and yelled "you don't belong here!" She was right. I didn't belong there. But I refused to let them intimidate me.

With my head held high, I strolled into *The Posh Market* and waltzed back to the meat department like I owned the place. Sure, people were pointing and whispering "it's him . . . that's him . . . the one from the car," while I was waiting in line, but I didn't let it bother me. Instead I made conversation with the nice elderly woman in front of me.

"So, what are you getting today?" she asked innocently enough.

"Italian sausage," I replied. "I'm making Sunday Gravy for my engagement party tonight."

"Well, bless your heart. Isn't that the sweetest thing," she said with a suspiciously nice tone. She then turned to the butcher and placed her order. "I want to buy all of the Italian sausage you have." She then turned back to me and added, "I'd rather buy it all just to throw it away than let it go to someone like you." She then shook her finger in my face adding, "You're not welcome here anymore."

After being threatened by an old woman, I decided to leave *The Posh Market* and search for Italian sausage elsewhere. The only problem was that my Camaro was lost in a sea of standard issue soccer mom luxury mini-vans with private school stickers in the rear windows. An hour later, I found my car and headed to the *Super Big-Mart,* where I bought an off brand Italian sausage that I'd hoped I could pass off as *Posh Market* sausage.

When I got back home and started making the sauce, it became obvious to me that the *Super Big-Mart* brand Italian sausage was going to be a problem. It was grainy in texture and it looked more like old hotdogs than sausage links. At that point it was too late to turn back though, so I had to press on with the ingredients that I had. I spent the rest of the day slowly simmering the Sunday Gravy, stirring it occasionally, adding seasoning when needed, taste testing as often as possible, and praying that no one noticed the inferior sausage.

Shortly before six o'clock, Fee reminded me that guests would soon be arriving for the party. As it was explained to me, the plan was simple. We would have everyone over for dinner, have a bite to eat, maybe even a drink or two, say "thanks for coming," and then call it a night. Well, that was the plan anyhow. And the plan sounded good. I liked the plan.

As I got dressed that evening, I went over the plan in my head one more time just to see if still sounded solid. To my best estimate it did. But as I stood in front of the mirror,   buttoning my comfort fit *Slacks*, it donned on me that I didn't have the first clue as to what the plan actually entailed. Since I had spent my entire day preoccupied with making the Sunday Gravy I never took the time to check my email to see who D-Love had invited.

So as I squeezed myself into my *Slacks* I yelled to Fee, who was in the other room getting ready, "Fee, who's coming tonight?"

Fee excitedly popped her head in the door to remind me, "Pookie, I'm so excited! You finally get to meet Troy! You're going to love Troy. He's the funniest guy ever! Everything he does is so funny! Oh, my god, I'm so excited!" and suddenly the plan lost its charm.

Ever since I'd met Fee, she'd talked about her friend, Troy, or as everyone knew him, Troy the Naughty Wizard. From what I could gather, Troy the Naughty Wizard wasn't a stage name or anything like that. He wasn't a magician. He wasn't an actor. He didn't even wear a wizard's costume. He just made everyone call him Troy the Naughty Wizard because he was obnoxious. Everything he did was obnoxious. He should have been Troy the Obnoxious Jerk.

"Great," I sighed. "Who else is coming?"

"Um," Fee began, "Let me see, all of the girls I work with and their husbands are coming. Plus Buttons, Bull, D-Love of course . . . oh, and I think your Cousin Leroy and his girlfriend are coming."

"Great," I sighed once again as I took one last look in the

mirror. Over the course of the next few minutes I tried my best to enjoy the quiet before the storm. But that was interrupted by a ringing of the doorbell, followed by Fee shouting, "Mac! Troy's here! Come in here and meet Troy!"

I left my bedroom and walked into the living room, where I met Troy the Naughty Wizard for the very first time. He wasn't at all what I'd pictured. For some reason, I assumed he'd be a little nerdy guy that hung out at comic book shops and played magic card games. But to my surprise, he was a big guy, built like a linebacker. He was well over six feet tall and from the look of it, just under three hundred pounds. But despite his own weight issues, the first thing he said was "Oh my God, you're fat," as he patted my stomach. He then continued adding the insults, saying, "How do you find the will to get out of bed in the morning?"

Not knowing what to say, I shrugged my shoulders. He then burst into a fit of laughter. "I'm just messin' with ya, man."

"God, Troy, you're so funny," Fee snickered. I somehow missed the humor. A few dozen fat jokes later, more guests began to arrive. Some of Fee's friends from work actually had manners and brought wine and desserts instead of hurtful comments about my weight. However, each time someone showed up with a dessert, Troy reminded everyone that I was fat, saying, "Well, I guess this tray of brownies is enough for Mac, but what about the rest of us?" Each of his brilliant quips was followed by an abundance of unrelenting laughter. Again, I failed to see the humor.

A few minutes later, Buttons and Bull arrived. I didn't get a chance to talk to them though. That opportunity was lost after a massive head butt from Buttons caused a momentary loss of speech capabilities. By the time I could regain focus enough to speak, they had moved on and were actively mingling amongst the other guests.

The last guests to arrive were Cousin Leroy and his girlfriend. Leroy brought a bag of *Crunchy Chips,* as usual, that he kept locked under his arm for most of the night. The only time he let them out of his sight was during dinner, while he inhaled three helpings of pasta and sauce.

Despite the fact that Troy the Naughty Wizard made endless

fat jokes at my expense, the night was going fairly well. After all, no one had eaten the sausage, so there were no complaints about the Sunday Gravy. I could only assume that Fee tipped everyone off to the fact that it was from *Super Big-Mart,* since not one single guest had tried it. I did though. I wanted to see if it was as bad as it looked . . . it was.

Halfway through dinner, Troy began tapping his glass with a fork in order to call everyone's attention. "Wow, this is real crystal," he began, "I'm surprised that Mac can afford it, since he spends all of his money on food," he concluded with an outburst of laughter. "I'm just messin' with ya, man," he said with a smile.

Fee then tapped my leg and whispered, "I told you he was funny."

"He sure is," I replied.

"Ok, so I'd like to make a toast," Troy announced. He then laughed before adding, "Sorry Mac, I'm not making toast, I'm making a toast." He then raised his glass and changed his tone of voice to a very serious one, saying, "Mac, I'd just like to say . . ." He then stopped in mid sentence and changed his train of thought. He then insisted that I stand next to him. "Come here, man, I want everyone to see you."

Even though I knew I would live to regret it, I still got up and walked to the other side of the table to stand next to Troy the Naughty Wizard. He threw his arm around me and very kindly said, "You're a good guy, Mac. You deserve a good girl. And over there," he said, pointing to Fee, "you got yourself a great girl."

Looking over at Fee, seeing how happy she was, made it a surprisingly sweet and touching moment. I looked back at Troy, who was standing there with his glass raised, and for the first time all night I saw him as a real person instead of a one dimensional obnoxious jerk. I couldn't believe it, but I was actually starting to warm up to Troy the Naughty Wizard. He then pulled me in closer and softly asked, "You know what we used to do guys like you in high school?"

Before I had a moment to even think about it, Troy yanked my pants down in front of everyone, yelling, "Oh snap! The naughty wizard strikes again!"

After getting pants-ed in front of my closest friends and a

few complete strangers, I decided not to talk to Troy for the rest of the night. Instead I spent the rest of the engagement party talking to Cousin Leroy about the awesomeness that is Chuck Norris. Listening to Leroy blab on endlessly about Chuck and all things Chuck related was like music to my ears compared to one more fat joke from Troy.

As things began to wind down, and the majority of the company had already left, I couldn't help but notice that as we talked, Cousin Leroy continued slowly but surely to inch his way to the kitchen. Before long, we were standing in the kitchen and Cousin Leroy had stopped talking about Chuck Norris altogether. Instead, he was focused on one thing and one thing alone; scouting out leftovers. At that point I knew it was just a matter of time before he began dropping hints that he wanted some of the leftovers.

"Dude, so where's yer tupperware?" he boldly asked.

"Ugh," I sighed. "In the left hand cabinet," I said, pointing to the cupboard. Leroy then proceeded to clean me out, taking every bit of the leftovers with him. When he finally left with three tupperware containers full of Sunday Gravy the night from hell was over . . . or so I thought. It wasn't until then that the *Super Big-Mart* Italian sausage decided to disagree with me and I spent the rest of the night vomiting uncontrollably. It was by far the most miserable experience of my life.

The next morning, after about twenty minutes of sleep, I awoke to Cousin Leroy banging on the door. He burst into the apartment and breezed right past me into the kitchen.

"Leroy, what's wrong?" I asked.

"Whew," he said in relief. "Found 'em."

"Found what?" I asked.

"I left my *Crunchy Chips,*" he said from the other room. He then emerged from the kitchen and said, "Dude, come have breakfast with me at *The Pancake House* so I can have some company."

-True Story. ❧

D-Love Moved My "Cheese"

One evening I was sitting on the couch, flipping through channels, just trying to find something good on television. When I first turned the television on, I didn't think that would be a very difficult task. After all, we were premium cable subscribers so we had over four hundred channels to choose from.

Mathematically speaking, "something good" was bound to be on television. However, after flipping through a few hundred channels of nothing but morally bankrupt reality shows, two things became painfully obvious. The first was that Mathematics was a worthless subject with no practical uses for everyday life. The second was that there was nothing good on television.

Once I accepted the harsh facts of life, I lowered my expectations and began searching for something that was just ok or maybe, even at the very least, mildly entertaining. When that too proved to be an impossible task, I figured I would settle for something . . . anything really . . . that was at least halfway tolerable. A few dozen channels later, I landed on *Who Wants to Marry My Celebrity Mom's Millionaire Midget Skating Partner?* and I realized that my expectations were still too high. Not willing to lower them any further, I laid down the remote and gave up my quest altogether. Not to mention, my thumb was getting tired from all the button pushing . . . I always had weak thumbs.

At that point, D-Love walked into the living room. He was carrying a paperback novel in one hand and a manila envelope in the other. As soon as he entered the room he tossed the manila envelope onto the coffee table and sat on the edge of the couch. He then reached over and picked up the remote control.

"It's not worth it," I warned him, holding up my injured thumb.

"Nobody cares about your gimpy thumbs," D-Love snarled as he turned off the television. "This is important," he concluded. He then closed his eyes and took a few deep breaths in order to focus himself. Then in dead silence, he just sat there as if trying to pick the perfect words to say. Clutching the paperback novel in his right hand, he reached out and placed his left hand on my shoulder as he very solemnly stated, "Mac, you need new cheese."

Not knowing what to say in response, I just stared at him blankly until he got the hint that elaboration of his previous statement was needed. After a rather tedious pause, D-Love held up the paperback book and firmly repeated, "Cheese, Mac. Cheese."

"Cheese?" I asked.

"Cheese," he repeated, yet again offering absolutely no insight into what he was talking about. Not until we went through a veritable "Who's on first?" routine did D-Love finally explain himself. Apparently he had just finished reading a motivational book about metaphorically significant cheese. Based on what he'd read, he came to the conclusion that it was time for me to make a career change despite the fact that I was more than content with my station in life . . . what with attaining the prominent position of Library Technical Assistant II and all. But as he explained it, I needed new cheese because "New cheese is good cheese and old cheese, even if it's good cheese at the time, is actually bad cheese."

Then he lectured me on the importance of various types of cheeses for thirty-seven minutes straight. I tried counting how many times he said "cheese" but I got bored and zoned out during most of what he was saying. I caught the basic gist of it, though.

Long story short, according to D-Love's interpretation of the book, it didn't matter that I was happy with my job. Rather what truly mattered most was making, "mo' cheddah." When his lecture eventually started winding down, I was finally able to get a word in.

"D, that's nice and all but I'm pretty set with the cheese that I have. So . . . sorry, I don't really want any new cheese," I explained.

"Oh, you don't want new cheese, huh?" D-Love shook his head. "Well that's too bad because you're getting new cheese and you're going to like it," he asserted. He then shook his finger, saying, "It's high time you get a job."

"I have a job," I reminded him.

"Oh, right, I forgot about your job at the library," he said using air quotes to emphasize the words "job" and "library." He then continued, adding "I'm talking about a real job, Mac. Fee and I have decided that it's time you left the library to pursue a more fulfilling career."

"What? When did you talk to Fee about this?" I asked.

"We've been planning this for weeks, Mac," he replied. "These things take time. We had to spice up your resume, post it on line, send it out, sift through the offers, play hard ball with salary negotiations . . . look, it's very technical," D-Love said as he stood up from the couch. He then picked up the manila envelope and added, "All you need to know is that you start tomorrow." He then flung the envelope at me and added, "Oh, and Fee wants you to wear the pink button down shirt to make a good impression."

There were a million questions racing through my head at that particular moment but the one I managed to ask was "What do you mean I start tomorrow? Start what?"

"Your new job in marketing," D-Love informed me.

"Marketing? How would I get a job in marketing? I don't know the first thing about marketing. Not to mention, I didn't even interview with a marketing company," I explained.

"Mac," he began with a disappointed look, "You just don't get it do you? With a resume like yours, you don't need to go through interviews. Jobs are just handed to you," he said as if I should have known.

"But I don't even have a good resume," I explained.

"You do now that we took care of it," D-Love replied using air quotes to emphasize the phrase, "took care of it."

"You took care of it?" I asked.

"Shyah . . . we took care of it," he said in a huff. "Are you even paying attention? We spiced it up, so you need to look it over to familiarize yourself with your work experience," he explained using air quotes to emphasize the phrases "spiced it up" and "work experience."

"What do you mean, you spiced it up?" I asked as I opened the envelope.

"Well . . . we made a few minor modifications and added some slight enhancements here and there. If you want good cheese, you need a good resume, Mac," he replied once again using air quotes to emphasize "minor modifications" and "slight enhancements."

"Seriously, the air quotes are getting on my nerves," I informed him.

"Sorry," he said using air quotes.

"Stop with the air quotes!" I yelled as I punched him in the face . . . in my mind. In reality I just gave him the evil eye as I pulled my "spiced up" resume out of the envelope. Upon taking an initial glance at my newly "spiced up" resume, I couldn't help but notice that D-Love was just a little too liberal with his "minor modifications."

"D, I can barely use a computer and this says I'm a certified Information Systems Engineer," I said, pointing to the list of "computer skills."

"Pfft," D-Love began, "you can turn a computer on, right? So I simply described your particular skill set with some more dynamic sounding terminology. It's no big deal. That's how you enhance a resume, Mac," he explained.

"Oh, well that sounds reasonable," I said, assuming he knew better than I did. However, I continued reading and found that he made a few rather unreasonable enhancements. For instance, under the section marked "work experience," Library Technical Assistant II was "spiced up" with the snappier sounding title of "South Carolina State Governor."

"D, this is the dumbest thing I've ever read," I bluntly stated. "Embellishing my computer skills is one thing, but South Carolina

State Governor? Come on. It would only take someone about three seconds of research to discredit that information." I said as I tossed the envelope back on the coffee table.

D-Love snatched it back up, pointed it at me and sternly said, "Listen, Mac, nobody checks these things. So don't get bogged down in the details. Just focus on tomorrow."

"Why, what's tomorrow?"

"You really don't pay attention to anything do you? You start your new job tomorrow, Mac," D-love reminded me.

"Oh right, my new job," I mockingly replied using air quotes to give D-Love a taste of his own medicine. It was sweet . . . sweet as in "it was satisfying to mock him," not sweet as in "the taste of his medicine was sweet" . . . never mind. It was still pretty sweet though.

After taking a moment to giggle to myself, I continued, "So if I'm starting a new job tomorrow, what am I supposed to do about the Library?"

"Call 'em up and tell 'em you quit," D-Love instructed.

"I can't just quit. I'm a keeper of . . ." I began only for D-Love to finish my sentence with, "of the Dewey Decimal System and the world would spin into a vortex of chaos if you didn't go to work, blah, blah, blah, I know. Just quit."

"Ok, fine. Let's suppose I quit. What would I be doing for this marketing company?" I asked.

"Ugh," D-Love sighed. "That's it, no more questions!" he barked.

"But I have a lot of questions," I insisted.

"No. No more. I'm done answering questions. All you need to know is that as of tomorrow you'll have new cheese. So quit the library or there will be consequences," he said using air quotes to emphasize the word "consequences." He then gave me an evil eye and began walking out of the room. But before he exited, he paused to add "Oh . . . and Fee wants you to wear the pink button down shirt." He then exited the room, walked down the hallway into his room and shut the door.

The next morning as I was ironing my pink button down shirt, I decided to take D-Love's threat to heart and quit my job.

Though I had no idea what D-Love meant by "consequences," I assumed quitting my job would probably be better than facing those "consequences." So I went into the living room and I called the library to tell them I was going to quit.

"Hey Ethel, this is Mac and I . . . " I began.

"Mike? Mike isn't here today," Ethel interrupted.

"Mike? No, I'm not asking for Mike. I'm telling you this is Mac," I explained.

"I don't know anyone named Mac. You must be talking about Mike. Mike isn't here," Ethel insisted.

"No, Ethel, no one named Mike works there. You're thinking of Mac . . . I'm Mac," I tried to explain.

"No, I'm pretty sure his name is Mike. And Mike isn't here today," she repeated. "Better luck next time," Ethel said before hanging up.

A few minutes later I called the library back in hopes of talking to someone who actually knew who I was. Fortunately Trevor answered the phone.

"Hello, Trevor, this is Mac," I began.

"Mike? Mike isn't here today," Trevor interrupted.

"Ugh," I sighed. "No, Trevor, I'm not asking to speak with Mike. I'm telling you, this is Mac. You know, Mac?" I asked in hopes of jarring his memory. However, just like Ethel before him, he insisted my name was Mike.

"No, I'm sorry, I don't believe anyone named Mac works here. You must be thinking of Mike. I don't believe he's in yet though," Trevor answered.

"Listen, Trevor, this is Mac. I'm a Library Technical Assistant. I've worked there for three years now and I've never missed a day of work . . . We eat lunch together in the break room at least four days a week . . . You're always insisting that I try whatever curried goat dish you're eating . . . Last week I passed out after smelling your homemade kimchee, remember?" I began growing impatient. "Come on! Mac! You know who I am. You have to. I've worked there for three years!" I shouted.

"Ah," Trevor sighed before taking a slight pause to add,

"You must be thinking of Mike."

"No, Trevor, I'm not thinking of Mike! I'm telling you my name is Mac!" I insisted.

"Do me a favor and hang on a second. I'll see if Mike has shown up yet," Trevor said before putting me on hold. A few minutes later, he picked back up and informed me that Mike had not yet shown up for work. "I'm sorry, Mike isn't in. Perhaps you could call back later," Trevor suggested.

At that point, I was a little steamed. I was having a hard time believing that none of my co-workers knew that my name was Mac and that the entire time I had worked there they all assumed my name was Mike. However, the mis-communication on the phone that morning did finally explain why the name plate on my desk said Mike.

"Listen, Trevor, for the last time, my name is Mac. No one by the name of Mike works there," I firmly stated.

"Yes, that's correct. Mike isn't here today, would you like to leave him a message?" Trevor asked.

"Ugh," I sighed. "No, that's ok. I'll call Mike later," I said before hanging up the phone. A few minutes later I called the library for what would be the third and final time. After a few dozen rings, Ethel answered the phone. She must have lost the coin toss.

"Library, this is Ethel," she answered.

"Ethel, hi, this is Mike," I began.

"Oh, hey, Mike. Someone just called looking for you. I didn't catch his name though," she interrupted.

"Yeah, that's cool," I sighed. "Listen, I'm calling to let you know that I'm not coming in today," I informed her.

"What? You're not coming in today?" Ethel asked with panic in her voice. I knew the panic wasn't out of concern for my well being. It wasn't a "You're not coming in? Oh my God, is everything ok?" tone of voice that she was using. Instead, I knew that she was mostly concerned with her lunch schedule.

She then continued freaking out and proved my point completely. "What do you mean you're not coming in today? If you don't come in today then who will cover the desk when I go to lunch?"

Completely disgusted with Ethel's selfishness, I finally did something I never thought I'd ever do in my life. I told her off . . . well, Mike told her off, but even though I was using a fake identity, it still felt pretty good.

"Listen, Ethel, I don't care when you go to lunch, because I quit," I proudly proclaimed.

"You quit? What do you mean you quit? Now the lunch schedule will be ruined. Why would you do that to me, Mike?" Ethel asked.

"Well, Ethel," I said, trying to sound as cool as possible, "D-Love moved my cheese." As the phone fell from my hand and went crashing to the floor, I realized that the moment may have been a bit cooler had I not attempted to use air quotes to emphasize the word "cheese." Oh well.

-True Story.